Other Titles
by Anita L. Allee

Historical Titles
Closed, Do Not Enter
Child of the Heart
Yankee Spy in New Orleans
Who's the Boss
Two Together
Mississippi River Road

Contemporary Title
Back Country Adventure

Watch for Future Publications.

About the Author:

Anita L. Gatson Allee, a life-long resident
of Missouri, grew up, one of four children
in rural northeastern Missouri, on a family farm.
She is a graduate of University of MO,
at Columbia, Missouri.
She has been married over fifty years
to the same husband,
mother of two grown daughters,
and five grandchildren from twenty-four
down to eight years of age.
She is a professional volunteer in
Christian activities and community affairs.

You may contact the author at:
Anita L. Allee
13268 Church Road
Versailles, MO 65084

or by e-mail at:
anviallee@earthlink.net

▲▲☼▲▲

God's Messenger

By Anita L. Allee

A Contemporary Novel
of
tragedy and triumph
of the human spirit, because of
personal reliance upon
their Savior.

Cover Painting by Mary King Hayden

Graphics Design by Linda Hamilton
of B & W Graphics

ISBN: 978-1-60458-609-1
Published by Anita L. Allee

Allee, Anita L.
Fiction-Title
Inspirational-Christian

Printed in the United States of America
by InstantPublisher.com

Dedication

These words were inspired by occurrences when one of the author's first cousins passed away only four and a half weeks after a diagnosis of cancer in major organs of his body.

At the time he breathed his last, a huge bull elk came down the mountain. This blessed his sisters who waited with him. They felt it was a message from God that their outdoors man brother was home in the arms of his Lord.

This is not his story, but his story led to this one.

This story was bathed in tears. I pray it can touch you and lead you closer to God with each breath you take and each word you read.

My own dear husband, Vincel Allee, passed during this same time.

Dedicated to Karl Wayne Gatson
and his sisters: Karolee, Kolleen, and Kathleen.

Disclaimer: This is a work of fiction, any references to the towns in Colorado and the Colorado State University are incidental.

The contamination incident in the storyline is totally fictitious.

Sigrid Noll Ueblacker, was the actual Founder of the Birds of Prey Foundation.

The balance of the characters in the story are figments of the imagination of the author.

Any errors are claimed by the author.

Scripture is from the KJV of the Bible or paraphrased

Story Characters

Timothy Scott Thayer - Young Forestry Student and State Forestry and Animal Research Employee

Lydia Brown Thayer - wife of Scott

Timothy Scott Thayer II - Couple's Young Son

Archie and Vera - Mountain Resort Owners

Sam and Drew - Scott's Friends and Fellow Employees

Miss Carmen - Lydia's Fellow Teacher and Friend

Joseph - University Research Professor and Scott's College Friend

Reverend Jeff Boyd - Despondent Minister on Sabattical Leave From His Church

Dixie - A Golden Retriever

Dr. Zach - Dixie's Former Owner

(Some of the peripheral characters are named for the children of a Pre-school Sunday School Class.)

God's Messenger

When Timothy Scott Thayer entered Colorado State University at Fort Collins, Colorado, September of 1993, he knew exactly what he wanted to do with his life. He had already worked at Scout Camps as an instructor of water craft and other outdoor sports; he had planted trees in the forests of Colorado and Canada; helped at a rehabilitation facility for injured wildlife; and been an all-round son. He was the only child of "Big" Scott Thayer, a supervisor at Pingree Park Campus, Mummy Range, fifty-three miles northwest of Fort Collins and alumnus of the same campus. Big Scott was one of the first fifteen hundred veterans from WWII who returned to college at Colorado A & M, later the college name was changed to Colorado State University, and the study of forestry and land management, to the Department of Forest, Rangeland and Watershed Stewardship.

His parents and grandparents imparted knowledge and love for God, the forest and lands in the Rocky Mountains of Colorado.

Scott's mother worked as one member of a raptor rehabilitation team for eagles and other birds of prey in the Rocky Mountains. They received birds from much of the outlying area and were world famous for their ability to return the big birds to the wilds. She traveled with several select birds that would never be returned to the wilds, due to permanent changes in their ability to hunt and exist. Her traveling companions included Ole Harry, a bald eagle, with only one wing; Hoot, a great horned owl, with only one eye and a severe dent in the middle of his face; a Peregrine Falcon that had lost a leg to a steel trap and numerous other smaller birds accompanied her entourage when she went to educate schools and gatherings. She taught about the benefits of all God's creatures in the balance of nature amongst the wilds.

Scott accompanied his mother and assisted in the care and fed her charges as long as he could remember. He held a special love for the raptors.

His mother's colleague was the founder of Birds of Prey Foundation, Sigrid Noll Ueblacker, taught with Scott's mother during annual bird rehabilitation seminars and workshops. Scott always assumed Sigrid was the "bird whisperer" for raptors.

During his five years at Colorado State University, CSU, Scott studied in the Canadian Rockies on one research venture, in Alaska, and at the Colorado Division of Wildlife at the Foothills Campus on the north west edge of Fort Collins.

He entered CSU shortly after the Hourglass Fire of 1994, and was involved in rebuilding in 1995. He was able to study the early stages of forest restoration and regrowth when the university students attempted to restore ponderosa pine forests lost to the crown fire. Lodgepole Pine and aspen had naturally replaced the old growth forests on south ridge after the destruction. Scott loved the aspen, but his studies indicated the older type forests were the best choice for south ridge.

While at the auxiliary campuses, Scott and his fellow students took the Challenge Ropes Course, the rock wall climbing area, and attempted to walk the five mountain hiking trails within twenty-four hours. They had previously walked each of the trails on many occasions and Scott regularly escorted tourists and Elderhostel participants during hiking programs.

These escorted tours required CPR and other first aid training. Physically he was in the best condition of his life.

The five hiking trails covered peaks from 11,000 to over 13,000 feet above sea level. Those not accustomed to the high elevation sometimes got themselves into trouble when they attempted too much activity after a short time in the mountains. It was Scott and the other guides' job to pace the newcomers so all participants remained safe and could enjoy their surroundings and the experience of the mountain forests.

Scott felt strength and exuberance during his years at the University. Doing exactly what he wanted did not seem like work to him.

During Scott's working trips to the forest campuses of CSU, he often saw a young woman painting amongst the cliffs and timber. She was usually on a promontory and looking upwards.

There's that beautiful angel again. Much of the time when I come to work in this part of the forest, I see her here painting the scenery. Today, she is standing there with her orange skirt billowing in the breeze. It dances like the fall coins on the aspen trees. I wonder what her subject is for today?

One of these days, I'm going to get nerve to climb up there and ask her name. I wonder what her face looks like? I like her autumn colored hair.

She is so intent on her subject, she is oblivious to us working. She looks up, not down at us mere ants working below her.

He turned to go.

Today, I'm all sweaty. I'll find a better time.

Stop it man, you're going to embarrass yourself and get these other guys interested and I definitely don't want that. I want to speak to her first.

One sunny day, he donned his hiking boots and marched purposely to her promontory.

He coughed before he stepped into the open to warn her of his coming.

"Hi, my name's Scott Thayer. I often see you painting and wanted to meet you. Hope you don't mind. I'm harmless. I work down there planting new trees." He indicated the slope below and across the valley.

"I know, I've seen you guys and gals on the slopes and campus," she said.

"I've never seen you on campus, but of course I didn't know what your face looked like, so if I had, I might not have known." Scott laughed, "I guess I'm running on too much, but all that is true."

"Yes, you look different close-up too. Seeing people's hats isn't a good introduction." She glanced at her watch. "I need to go, I have a class this evening."

"May I walk you back to your car?" he asked.

"Not this time. Besides you just got here, you may

want to stay longer." She gathered her belongings and folded her easel.

"That's pretty awkward to carry, don't you need help?" Scott asked.

"No, by now, I'm accustomed to carrying my paint equipment. I've developed a system." She turned and fled.

Scott watched her go. He saw her dump a rock from her shoe at the first bend in the trail.

She didn't look back.

Probably scared her to death. He banged his forehead. *I didn't get her name. Gotta do better next time.*

"Mike, do you know the auburn-haired woman who paints in the mountains above where we are planting those trees?" Scott asked one of his art student friends.

"You might mean Lydia, but she's not available," Mike replied.

"Is she married, or engaged?" Scott asked.

"No, but she turns down everyone who asks her out. I even asked her. She goes with a group for coffee or painting, but that's about all we get from her," Mike said. "I don't think she's taken. She lives in the dorm."

"Do you know her name?" Scott asked.

"Yeah, I think her last name is Brown, Lydia Brown. Yeah, that sounds right. Not many take roll in our classes but I believe that's it. She rooms with Marti Pearson. I see her next hour, I'll ask her for Lydia's name and number. What do you want to know for?" Mike asked.

Scott looked down. "Why do guys usually want the name and phone numbers of women? You figure it out."

"Okay, I'll stick this note to the front of my portfolio. I'll get back to you after class. And, remember, fellow, you owe me one!" Mike crowded.

"I will and I will pay up too. How about dinner tonight

at my folks?" Scott said.

"Wow, I get to go for a home cooked meal. That is a good pay off. Do you want any other favors while I'm at it?" Mike asked.

"This one will do for now. Thanks, pal." Scott turned to walk away. "I better get cracking if I'm going to have your dinner ready in time."

"You mean you're cooking it? This may not be such a bargain after all," Mike said.

"It is. My mommy taught me to cook and I can turn out a mean steak. You won't regret it." Scott waved as he hurried down the steps from the student union.

It required several attempts for Scott to entice Lydia to have a coffee break at the Union, but his persistence paid off. Soon, they became an item around campus and on the slopes.

The pair spent many of their early dates walking around the Oval in the center of campus. Their walks provided them the opportunity to be out in a bit of nature. The Oval had a park-like setting, paved road and some of the oldest buildings on campus formed the outside perimeter of the Oval. It provided a "cheap date" for the couple who had little extra money to spare.

They also hung out on study dates at the Morgan Library and caught a quick soda and burger at Lory Student Center.

As spring advanced, they went to the mountains.

Scott was often away from the campus on research projects. He was gone during the July "Spring Creek Flood of 1997."

On a summer internship, Lydia rode out the flood in her second floor dorm room away from the water caused by two days of downpour in west Fort Collins. All students survived, but the campus suffered 200 million dollars worth of damage and the couple lost the library and student center for some of their inexpensive dates on campus.

The young couple endured remodeling and rebuilding during the year of 1998-1999. Being near graduation, neither was greatly hampered in their movement toward the spring commencement 1999.

In the early spring, Scott proposed in the middle of the lake Granby, while taking Lydia for a canoe ride.

They married in June, right after graduation.

New Home

Scott's new job stationed the couple on his favorite mountain to care for the wildlife and forests. He claimed the mountain as his own. Scott looked at the mountain above their chosen home site. "Lord, like Caleb in Joshua 14:12, I ask for this mountain. If it's in your will, give me this mountain for our home, my work and my family."

Scott and Lydia acquired a small acreage near the base of the mountain where they started to build their dream log house with their own hands while they lived in a tent during the summer. During the winter, they lived in the portion of the cabin they had finished. At first, only the kitchen, small laundry room, the open living room, and the master bedroom and bath, were all they needed.

Their first fall, Scott's research project was to assist with the annual late summer Bison and Elk Round-Up in the Yellowstone Basin. Forestry and conservation workers, and students assisted with the gathering of blood samples and physical data for the herds. The captures occurred when the summer calves were old enough to handle the stress and before the animals dispersed from the summer pastures.

Conservationists, environmentalists, and ranchers had battled for years over the possibility of disease being spread from the herds to their cattle herds and back again. Knowledge would lead to preventative measures and the collected data gave the researchers that information.

This was Lydia's first field trip with her new husband. She painted and watched the procedures, while the crew worked.

Lydia recorded the mountains around the pasture basins, the animals, and the crew as they worked.

During the evenings, they had time alone or with the crew, whichever they choose. It was a continued honeymoon for the newly married couple.

"Lydia, your new painting looks like the western artist, Russell. You've got the animals like he captured in his paintings. The only thing, you missed that one wreck with Joe today," Scott said.

"I wasn't fast enough. I had this started and by the time that occurred, the space was taken. I worry about you guys. It would be so easy for someone to be injured when you're working with such large animals," Lydia said.

"We all get banged up a bit, but with the tranquilizers, most of the animals are fairly well down by the time we move in. That one was a *doozy*. After the second dose, we gave up. The vet was afraid we'd kill him, rather than do our harmless tests," Scott said.

"It looked pretty dangerous to me from up on the rocks," Lydia said.

"Dealing with live animals, or people, they're all different. You never quite know what their reaction may be. We use a lot of ropes from different directions, so we do have checks and balances in case things don't go as expected. We trust each other and that's a very important part for our safety," he said.

"I can see you trust each other, but still, I don't want you to get hurt, or anyone else either," she said.

"This is important to the animals and all the people involved. If the cattle hadn't infected the wild stock with brucellosis and then back to the cattle in return, this wouldn't be necessary. The wild animals have developed a secondary immunity, but that doesn't mean the cattle can withstand a return attack. The possibility of wasting disease also makes the ranchers wild. In the long run, the animals would all be slaughtered. We're trying to find a better means of control, so everyone will be happy, or at least do the right thing," Scott said.

"I know it's important, but I'll offer a little prayer too," Lydia said. She reached to hug Scott. "I just found you, I don't want to lose you now."

"You won't. I'm tough and I find this work very exhilarating," he whispered.

"I can tell you all do. Some of that must be that man thing we so often are taught about in psychology classes," she replied.

"Well, you notice the gals don't back down either," he said.

"Yeah, but it isn't a game to them. You guys do your war dances, but the gals take care of the details. Ever notice that? The gals do a lot of the detail work," she said.

"Is that why they scream so loud when we capture the next animal?" he asked.

"Could be. Or it might be they're just a little smarter than the guys and know how to protect themselves better," Lydia said.

"You protected yourself, but I've got you now." He caught her around the waist and pulled her against him.

"I'm not running."

Home on the Mountain

The cabin was two-story and had many details which made the home very comfortable, but also simple in appearance. Their mountain-stone fireplace leaped to a ceiling two-stories high.

Scott used some of the trestle-style of Old Faithful Inn for the stairway and beam construction. Some of his college buddies from forestry school came to help with the overhead beams. All enjoyed spending some summer hours camping and enjoying the out of doors. Some of their friends already had a young child or two.

Lydia and Scott dreamed of the day a baby would add to their lives.

Scott and Lydia had been definite, they wanted a large window wall with a view of "their" mountain and the trails they loved to climb. The animals constantly traversed the trails coming and going to the lower meadows. Some ventured into their yard and close to their home.

Scott and Lydia had a blessing service for their home when it was mostly complete. Their friends from church and other neighbors attended. Scott read Psalms 127:1-3 from his CEV Scripture. "Without the help of the Lord, it is useless to build a home or to guard a city. It is useless to get up early and stay up late in order to earn a living. God takes care of his own, even while they sleep. Children are a blessing and a gift from the Lord."

Vera led the group in singing "Bless This House, oh Lord, we pray, make it safe by night and day. . ." The group applauded their own efforts when they completed the last verse.

Scott stepped up to paraphrase Psalm 127's first few verses. "Unless the Lord builds the house, the workers labor in vain."

Their pastor offered the final blessing. "Referring to Numbers 6 and verse 24, when the Lord spoke to Moses and directed him to bless the houses of Israel. 'May the Lord Bless you and keep you, may the Lord make His face to shine upon you and be gracious to you; The Lord lift up His countenance upon you, and give you peace.' Amen. Congratulations."

The crowd chorused their "Amens."

Scott raised his hands. "We can't thank you enough. You slaved here for these last few weeks to get us under cover by winter. Lydia and I appreciate it. That tent is getting a little cool. Thank you. Now, come and eat up, we've got goodies for a celebration. It's laid out on the deck, help yourselves."

When Scott and Lydia went down their mountain, the little community possessed, their friends Archie and Vera's resort, a small general store, and a community church. There were few neighbors during the winter, but the summer brought visitors and fall brought hunters to their mountain.

During Lydia's pregnancy, she made an art quilt to hang on their expected baby's wall. She included natural items, a twig, or a feather. She painted and stitched a sunrise, all from their mountain.

They wanted to be surprised when their baby was born, so she included the pinks and blues of the sky, sunrise, and sunset. A month before time of delivery, Scott hung the quilt on the baby's room wall.

"We're ready, just a little more time. We've got all the little items and paraphernalia we will need," Lydia said.

On their big day, they went down the mountain for the delivery of their firstborn, a son, named Timothy Scott Thayer the second. They called the baby Timmy. They assumed his name would evolve to Tim as he grew older.

At first the baby slept in a crib in their bedroom, then moved to his upstairs bedroom when it as completed and he was nearly two years old. He so loved his room, the move wasn't a difficult one. He moved himself when Scott installed his new big boy bed. Timmy could hardly climb the steps by himself, but he insisted on trying and made the effort several times each day.

Gradually they finished the large front porch the width of the front of the cabin, and a back porch with covered roof and deck at second-story level. The little boy especially liked to play in an area where they added a sand pile enclosed in one end. The railing provided a safe containment for him to play just outside their kitchen door.

Over the next couple of years, they planted nut trees and naturally-grown food producing plants in convenient places for their forest visitors.

When Timmy was three, Scott built an arch for Lydia over their front gate for her roses. They placed a two-rail fence around a portion of their lawn, along with some natural rock walls. These were not to keep the animals in or out, but to add to the appearance of their property. They insisted that all additions appear to have grown there naturally. The cabin fit into the natural setting and grew to be their world.

Happiness abounded, with everything they could have wished.

Each fall when the aspens colored, Scott went to the mountains to hunt and watch the changes in the forest. The forestry and animal research crews were worn-down by the end of their busy summer season and watching the forests gave respite to their worn bodies.

Father and Son

He took his little boy with him the fall Timmy was three. When he went alone, Scott had a rifle on the sling on his back, but he seldom took it off. When Timmy was along, he took only a holstered pistol and no plans to fire a round.

Scott's job required him to reside in his district all year. The couple began plans to home school their son because of difficulty in daily trips down off the mountain during winter months.

Lydia was a qualified teacher, so the educational process would not be difficult for them. They hibernated as a family during the winter, Scott went out on snowshoes to check the trails and do some work. Mom and Timmy sometimes walked out with him for shorter distances.

They kept two snowmobiles in case of emergency or the need to travel faster than they could walk. They had a generator for their electrical needs, should the power go off, and their source of heat was the forest in which they resided. Should they need to be gone, they had an auxiliary heat source.

Their neighbors, Archie and Vera, ran a mountain resort during the summer and the hunting season. The older couple saw after the Thayer cabin if the couple had to be gone for more than one night.

The entire family enjoyed the animals. Lydia continued to paint. She sold a few of her scenery paintings through their friends' resort.

With their baby, she added portraits of her own family to her paintings, either in outdoor scenery, or as individual portraits. Young Timmy was her favorite subject. Instead of photos around the house, they had paintings of each stage of the little boy's life.

From the day he was born, Scott talked to Timmy as if he were a man. Even when the little boy couldn't understand, Scott talked.

As time advanced, Timmy did understand.

"I expect great things from you. God gave you a good mind. I don't know what you'll choose to do with your life, but even if it's digging ditches, remember to do it for God and do a good job," Scott said.

Timmy didn't understand all his Daddy said, but he agreed and said, "Daddy, I think I'll do what you do."

"That would be fine, but it's okay if you want to do something different. You and God can do anything," Scott prompted his young son. "Take care of Mommy, she's going to take care of you too."

On one occasion the little boy got out on the limb of a tree and then was afraid to come down.

Scott held out his arms. "Jump to me, I'll catch you," he said.

"Daddy, I'm afraid. What if you miss?" Timmy asked.

"I love you, I won't let you fall. Let go. Let God and me catch you," Scott said. "Even when I'm not here to help, God loves you even more than I do. He wants what is best for you. He's going to take care of you, even if I'm not standing beside you."

Timmy's fingers got whiter, and whiter. He clung with his last bit of strength.

"Daddy, I can't hold on any longer!"

"I'm here, let go."

Timmy's last grip loosened and he fell into his Daddy's waiting arms.

"Told you so," Scott grinned.

Timmy's grin was bigger. "You did. So did God."

*   *   *

Scott and Timmy went to the forest often.

"Look, Daddy, there's a kitty," the little boy whispered as he tugged at his father's sleeve.

"That's a lynx, it's much bigger than a cat. Look it's got a bobbed-tail too and spots. Its fur is very soft. I'll show you one at the ranger station the next time we go down the mountain," Scott whispered.

"What's he doing?" Timmy asked.

"I'd say he's hunting for ground squirrels. He probably saw one go under that downed tree. He's like a big cat waiting for it to come back out. If it does, he'll make a nice lunch," Scott said.

"He'd eat a squirrel?" the little boy asked.

"That's right. God provided food for all His animals and sometimes that food is another animal. You like hamburgers don't you and hot dogs? One time, those were living critters too," Daddy said.

"Really, they were live animals? I don't want to eat any of the animals," the boy said.

"God said we were to have *dominion over all the earth*, that means we take care of the animals and the land. That's why I try to help take care of all the trees and the animals on our mountains. That means we can eat some of the animals, but we are to treat them well and be merciful in our care of them."

"Mur-ci- what?" Timmy asked.

"Merciful, means to be kind, or nice to the animals and to people. Give them good care," Scott said.

The family played in the lake each summer. Scott took Timmy into deeper and deeper water. He had practiced holding Timmy and jumping from the bank into waist high water. Scott gradually acclimated the little boy to holding his breath when they jumped in. At first, they didn't go under water, but water splashed into their faces.

"Hold your nose and this time, we'll go under the water," Scott said.

Timmy grabbed his nose, as he'd been taught and said, "Ready."

"Okay, here we go," Scott went under and came back up immediately.

Scott wiped his hand down the little boy's face. "Now, hold it longer and don't take your fingers off your nose until we come up out of the water. Okay, here we go, get ready," he said.

The pair moved a couple of feet under water and popped up again.

"Daddy, that was fun, do it again," Timmy yelled.

The pair increased the depth of their dives and the length of time they stayed under.

When Lydia came down, she was amazed to see the trust and fun the pair had going for them.

"Timmy, did you know you can open your eyes under the water and see fish and things?" she asked.

"Keep your eyes closed until we go down, then open them. When I get ready to bring you up, close them again," Scott said. "Let's practice with my hand under your chest and you putting your face into water. Here goes, close your eyes and hold your nose."

Timmy obeyed and they repeated the exercise often.

"Daddy, I saw a fish. He's over under the limb that hangs in the water. Can I get my pole and catch him?" Timmy asked.

"Sure, let's give it a try and see if he'll bite," Scott said.

Today, Lydia and Timmy walked to Vera and Archie's while Scott was in the mountains. Archie allowed Timmy to play with his hammer on the front porch.

Lydia talked while Vera peeled potatoes.

"We are going to home school Timmy when he's a bit older. That way, we won't have to worry about our depth of snow. We'll get all the equipment and supplies we need for the winter. Scott always gets plenty of firewood stockpiled, so we'll hibernate if the snow gets too deep. We have plenty of gasoline for the generator and the two snowmobiles if we have an emergency or need more supplies. I think we'll be all set. I'll wait until after Christmas and then start Timmy into some pre-school work. We'll have videos for part of his lessons."

She continued, "It's not like I haven't taught before. I think it will be fairly easy until Timmy gets to algebra, then his Dad can take a turn.

Archie and Timmy came inside for a drink of water.

Vera piped in, "Sounds like a winner to me. You've a wonderful little boy. You'll have lots of time to mix with other boys and girls in a few years. If you get into trouble, call on Archie. He always helped our boys with their homework. He got pretty good at it too."

Archie grunted, "I graduated when our youngest did. Don't you remember Vera?"

"That's what you said, but I know you'd never turn our Timmy down if he was in need," Vera added.

Lydia chuckled. "We'd better get back. Daddy will be home soon and he'll be hungry. He left very early this morning to observe the turkeys when they came off the roost. He wanted to see how many of that clutch survived the summer. He saw one of them go to bed last night and he wanted to be there when they came off the roost this morning. I think he's going to try to net some tomorrow to put radio collars on a couple of them."

Lydia looked at her son, "Timmy, he said he'd take

you along, if you can be very, very quiet. I might go too. We'd stay in the blind he set up two nights ago, but we'd have to go out very, very early. I'd have to wake you. Would you rather sleep tomorrow morning?"

"No, no, I want to go see the turkeys," Timmy shouted.

"Well, you'll have to be a lot quieter than that, if Daddy hopes to catch anything in his net," Lydia stated.

"Wow, that'll be good. I can hardly wait to see if he figured out where they went to roost tonight." Timmy said. "Can he put out his net tonight?"

"If Daddy found the roost tonight, he'll call some of his crew and they'll set up the nets by the bait he's been putting out. He has a blind. We and the crew will hide there. If you're not awake, we'll carry you up and wake you before dawn when the turkeys begin to move," Lydia said. "Bye, Vera and Archie. As you can see, we've got big plans for tomorrow."

Archie chuckled, "Let us know how it comes out."

"Sure, see you," Lydia said.

"See yah," Timmy mimicked.

Archie and Vera waved. They both had smiles on their faces.

Turkey Trap

The netting plans proceeded as outlined. Timmy was awake when they started up the mountain but he drifted off in the blind.

Later, Lydia put her finger over his lips and touched the boy's shoulder. Timmy jerked up quickly, "Did. . . .?

"Shh," Mom signaled.

She turned him to the screened window of the blind.

They watched silently.

The first turkey called and they heard him ruffle his feathers and flap his wings. The flock dropped out of the trees one by one. They were young and didn't fly long distances, but they were growing quickly.

The bulk of the flock gathered at the bait. Scott fired the cannons that flung the nets over the turkeys. The crew of three men rushed from the blind to further entangle the turkeys before they could injure themselves or escape. When all were secured, Lydia and Timmy went from the blind to the imprisoned turkeys.

"You missed two, Daddy," Timmy noted.

"But we got most of the young. I only need two. I think I'll take this young Jake gobbler and that hen. You fellows can put the collar on the hen and I'll get this gobbler. Lydia and Timmy, can you come and stand on the net on either side of him and I'll fasten his collar," Scott directed.

"Good, that's perfect. I don't want to hurt him but I have to have him still so he won't hurt himself and I can fit the collar so he can wear it until the battery runs out." He wrapped the orange plastic collar around the gobbler's neck, checked the size, then applied the small radio transmitter around the collar.

"There, he's all set. Men, how are you doing?" Scott asked.

"We got her ready to go. Do you want to check the collars before we turn them loose?" Sam asked.

"Sure do, I'll get the wands from the blind. Hang in there a little longer." Scott brought the two wands and tried each of the controls. Both poults transmitted the ping signals.

"Okay, let's ease up on them and get them untangled, then we can let the bunch go," Scott said. "Be careful not to get the radio or transmitter caught in the net."

"Son, you and Mom step back. Let her go," Scott

swung up one side of the net. The men lifted their portions and the birds ran and flew, then drifted into the timber.

Scott picked up a wand and one of the crew gathered the other. They quickly checked to be certain all equipment still functioned.

"Good here. How about yours?" Scott asked.

"Fine, she's giving a strong signal. I could find her right now, if I could run fast enough, but that's not likely. She'll be cagey and wild for a time now, but we won't need to catch her again, unless we find her stationary, then we might need to check to be sure she's still alive," Sam stated.

"Next spring, we can see if she's setting. Only half of them make it through the winter, so one of our two should statistically make it. Well, let's fold up the blind and get down for some coffee. You guys up to some ham and eggs?" Scott asked.

The crewmen laughed.

"Do we ever turn down a hearty breakfast when we are out before dawn and traipsing up mountains?" Drew asked.

"I'm ready right now, bring it on," Sam commented.

Scott didn't get to see the turkey hen set in the spring. That fall, he complained of being short of breath and having a pain in his right chest. They didn't think it was his heart, it was the wrong side, but he weakened.

Their local doctor took x-rays.

"I'm concerned about some shadows I see in your lung. We need to send you to Denver for a complete physical."

Scott and Lydia looked at each other.

"If that's what you think is best," Scott said. "I'm having trouble breathing. That won't do with me working in the mountains at high elevations and being out this winter."

They left the office.

"Lydia, I didn't like the way he looked after he checked out the x-ray," Scott said. "I think he saw something he's not telling us."

" Let's not worry until we see the specialists and see what they have to say. They know more about such problems than our regular doctor," Lydia said. She turned away to pretend to look across the street, *Oh, God, I'm scared. Please don't let Scott be sick. Help us, everything has been so perfect. I can't even think about anything happening to him.*

Timmy had stayed with Archie and Vera. His parents did not come home for four days.

The diagnosis was not good.

When they reached the cabin, Lydia settled Scott by the fire. He was still exhausted and recovering from multiple biopsies.

Lydia went down to pick up Timmy.

When she got to the resort, Vera was in the office, Archie and Timmy were out back.

"What's the verdict?" Vera asked.

Lydia could not speak. Tears welled and ran down her cheeks.

"Oh, baby, what can I do for you?" Vera asked.

"I'll tell you in a minute. Right now, I can't," Lydia cried.

Vera enfolded her in a hug and patted Lydia's back.

"I had to try to keep from crying before Scott, but I've got to let it out, just for a little bit," Lydia continued.

"Whenever or whatever you want to tell me, you can," Vera said.

"They did a bunch of biopsies. He has terminal cancer. It started in his lung. They checked the lymph nodes. It has already spread all over his body. They want to try some chemo to give him a little time, but we were so devastated, we had to come home and think about it. We'll have to go back on Monday to get started, if that's what we want to do," Lydia said.

"Do you know what you are going to do?" Vera asked.

"Yes, we are going to go for the treatment. Scott wants to do some video tapes for Timmy for later. He wants to fight it as long as he can. He's worn out now and I left him before the fireplace in his recliner. He was looking at the mountain when I left, but I think he was about to go to sleep. I need to get back pretty soon, but I had to tell someone. You tell Archie, I can't talk about it now, maybe when we see how things go."

Lydia continued, "Pray for a miracle, that's what we need and the only thing that will help. If Scott gets along well on the chemo, they think he might have three months. That might get us through the winter and to spring. I'm hoping they are wrong and he will improve, or the chemo will work much better than they think."

She added, "We don't know if it will make him sick, so we don't know how Timmy will take it. If Daddy is sick, it will be harder on our son too. I called Scott's parents and my parents, they will come later, but they want to give themselves and us a little time to adjust before they show up. They want to help, not make it worse for Scott."

Lydia sniffed, " I can't imagine how it will affect his parents. Scott is their only child and they love him beyond measure. He's been a wonderful son to them. They have been pleased with the work he does, with our marriage, and their only grandson."

She continued without a break, "I had hoped we'd have more children, but that hasn't happened. I regret we weren't able to give them more grand babies."

Lydia doubled over and sobbed. The whole situation bore her down.

Vera held her again. "Come, let's sit on the sofa. You rest a minute. I'll make you a cup of tea."

She returned with the tea and sat beside Lydia.

"Do you want us to keep Timmy another night?" Vera asked.

"No, I think his Daddy needs to see Timmy. I'll get hold of myself in a minute. We better get back. Scott is not feeling well after all the biopsies. They poked holes all over his trunk. Those and the verdict took a lot out of him. He may need something," Lydia said. "I brought along my sunglasses. I'll put those on and think of something to talk about with Timmy as we go up our mountain to our home," Lydia broke again. "I'm a mess. I need to get hold of myself. Scott doesn't need a blubbering idiot and Timmy certainly doesn't either."

"It's understandable, but you're right. You don't want to scare Timmy until you've had time to absorb all this and know how to tell him," Vera said. "Hospice was very helpful for me. You don't have to be dying to talk to them, but they can help you know how to tell Timmy and how to best handle all the adjustments you all are going to make with Scott's treatment. They are in the business and do this all the time."

"I hate to bother others, but I am going to need help." Lydia hugged Vera. "Thank you for giving me something positive I can do. I'll contact them when we go back to Denver in a few days. I felt so helpless and now at least I'll have one thing I can try. I'll go get Timmy now and we'll go back up the mountain to Scott. He's going to wonder what happened to us. I don't want to leave him alone for long, especially now. He has a lot on his mind. He's already worried about how Timmy and I will manage without him. I don't want him to get discouraged and give up. That's admitting defeat, and with God, I refuse to let us give up. Pray for us."

Lydia walked toward the door. She detoured to Vera's sink and splashed her face with cold water. She got a couple of ice cubes from Vera's ice maker and held them to her eye lids. "I'm pathetic. Forgive me Vera for unloading on you."

"Never you worry about that girl. I'm here for you anytime you need me. I've been through this and anytime you want to talk, give me a call, or come on down. I can send Archie up to Scott if you need a break, or I'll come myself and bring my knitting. I'm a very good sitter, you know. Archie will be happy to help out with anything you need done outside. Scott won't feel like doing much, so don't hesitate to ask us. We love you all, Timmy, Scott, and you too. God knows what is best, but I sure wish we knew His plans now. It buffaloes me to even think about it."

Lydia stepped from Vera's door, reached for her sunglasses from atop her head. She eased them to her face and dropped the ice cubes into Vera's flower bed.

"Timmy." She cleared her throat and tried again. "Timmy, we need to go home and see Daddy. Tell Archie thanks and let's go."

Their little boy raced ahead of her up the trail.

I'm glad he's gone on ahead, I don't feel like talking now. I'm afraid I might reveal some of my thoughts to our little man. I wish he could stay happy forever.

Oh, Lord, give me strength, help us all stand what is here and what is coming. Please heal Scott. I can't accept the diagnosis yet, help me to follow You, no matter where You lead. Bless Scott, keep him free from pain and bless Timmy. Let our little boy have his Daddy, if You possibly can.

The Fight of Our Lives

Vera approached Lydia the second day after Scott's diagnosis. "We'll take care of Timmy any time you need us. When you go for treatment, or if things get too bad at home, any time, remember that. We're serious. Timmy fits right in with both of us and we really want to do this for you all."

Lydia choked back tears, "Vera, you don't know how much this means to us. I have no idea how to handle any of this, but knowing we have support is a true blessing for us. Someday, when I can talk about this, I want you to tell me how you handled the illness, and. . . all with your first husband. I've not experienced anything like this and have no idea where to start," Lydia whispered.

"Please tell our pastor. I don't have the strength to go talk to him now, but tell him I'll be down when we get things a bit under control," Lydia said.

Vera gave her a hug. Anytime I can be of help, come down and we'll have a gab. Archie can help too, or we'll make it a *ladies' only* with a cup of tea."

"Now, I have to try to stay strong for Scott, but I feel like I'd fly into a million pieces if I gave in at all. I don't know what I'm doing half the time and the other half, I wish I didn't know what was going on," Lydia said.

"I know, there will be times like that, but God will get you through it and we're here to do what we can," Vera replied.

*   *   *

Shortly after his diagnosis was fully confirmed by the results of all the tests, Scott went to the mountain to spend time with God's creation and to come to terms with his prognosis. He had already passed through his time of shock, then denial, and guilt at the fact he would leave his family to fend for themselves through very crucial times in their lives.

He needed to work out his anger at the possibility of his life being cut short for him. During his time in the mountain, he wrestled with God, but ultimately, God's peace settled over him, with the exception of his concerns over the welfare of his family.

Oh, Lord, protect me from fear. Don't let my illness torture my family. Seeing them suffer over my illness, will be harder than being in pain myself.

He left the trail when he got back down to their cabin, then turned to look back up the mountain.

I wish I could stay here forever, but I need to be home to help Lydia and Timmy accept my being sick. . . maybe my going.

Scott returned from the mountain with a renewed sense of God's presence.

Lydia had watched for hours. She went out the door and looked into his face when he stepped up on their deck. "You seem at peace," she commented.

"I accomplished what I went for," he said. "I've found rest in God. He's in control and I will do what I need to. At the moment, I'm to love you and Timmy."

He continued, "I want to do some videos for him in case I won't be here. I want to do them when I'm feeling the best I can, so they won't also be a torment. After all that, I'm to take my medicine and do what the doctors say. I'll let God give us an answer," he said. "I will stay around as long as God allows." He hugged her to him, "I love you, I don't ever want to leave you, but I may not have that determination to make."

Lydia was quiet for a moment. "I need to lean on Him too, but right now, I can't take it all in. I'm not ready to stop fighting. I'm with you whatever you need to do," she said, "but I don't want you to go."

He hugged her tighter. "I know the answer may be that I need to go. That's all right, if that's what God says. He already knows I want to stay with you and Timmy, but I've put it into His hands. Scripture tells me, I need to lean on Him constantly, I can't do it myself."

Doctors and Hospitals

The specialist in Denver provided for the local hospital to administer the prescribed chemotherapy near their mountain, but once per month, they made the trip back to Denver for evaluation and further prescriptions.

The first month passed with little change. Scott and Lydia began to hope things would be better than predicted.

Another month, and then another of chemo treatment passed without signs of anything good occurring within Scott's body. Tests showed new growth, rather than shrinkage of the scattered tumors.

Many times, Scott was unable to eat and had no appetite for the most enticing meals.

Scott began to study and prepare to tape his messages for his son.

When he relaxed in his chair on the deck, Timmy cuddled against him.

Scott told his son many stories of his younger life, and about his grandfather and grandmother and their work. Scott made a point to tuck Timmy in at night and read him bedtime stories. They cuddled and spent many hours laying together in Scott's recliner in the evenings.

After Timmy went to bed, Lydia said, "If we didn't know you are sick, this would be the best time in our whole married life. We've never had you all the time and completely."

"I know, why do we wait to do the things we should until we nearly miss out? I've never been so close to Timmy before." His voice caught. "I've so enjoyed exploring his mind and personality. I know him in a way I haven't before. He's a great kid, if I do say so myself," Scott said.

"You seem so relaxed and he senses that. He knows you want to be with him and there are no distractions," Lydia commented.

"I wish we could have had that other baby we wanted," Scott mused.

"Me too, but God didn't give us that gift. There must be a reason," she whispered.

"Maybe you could still get pregnant," he said.

"Do you feel like making love?" she asked.

"Yes, I can't hold you close enough. Somehow it reminds me I am still alive," he whispered.

The next day, Scott was more himself. He reminded Lydia, "I've made it three months, I'm champing at the bit for the next round. I don't want to have any regrets about not doing all I can. If there is anything medically that can be done, I am going to try," Scott declared.

Lydia looked at him with great love shining in her face.

Scott pulled her to him and whispered in her ear, "God and I chose you. That was perfect. Timmy came into our lives and that was perfect. I want you to know it was all perfect and I thank you and God, no matter what happens from here on out."

Between their trips for chemo and three days of being deathly ill after each trip, Scott sequestered himself in their bedroom. He dictated his thoughts to the video camera Lydia set up for him. He asked her to leave him alone for these sessions. He had thoughts he wished to leave for Timmy and some for her, but didn't want to be more emotional than necessary. In her presence, he tried valiantly but sometimes was unable to hide his pain and frustration.

"Eat something, Scott. You've got to have strength for every fight," Lydia pleaded.

"It comes back. I don't want to expend all the energy I have trying to force something down, and then having dry heaves for an hour. Give me a graham cracker," Scott said.

Just when it seemed he was making progress, another treatment loomed. A repetition occurred of the last treatment with more sickness and down time. In a couple of days, he would rally and frantically get back to his self-appointed task of videoing all he wished to say to his family.

He labeled the tapes, one for each year until Timmy reached his twenty-first birthday. He covered every topic he could think of that would occur in a young man's life. In each tape, he told Timmy that he'd like to be with him, but if he had to go to heaven, he wished to leave messages.

In a video, Scott directed, "Timmy, go to God first, then Archie or your grandfathers if you have questions or problems your mom can't answer or handle."

He attempted to impart and spell out his personal values and what he wanted for Timmy.

He spent some hours telling his son about his own childhood and how he had learned many things from his parents and while in college. The last tape he made for Timmy was on fatherhood.

He told the little boy, "Outside of following God, and marrying your mother, being a father is the greatest thing in my life. I love you. You make me very proud to be your Daddy. Don't ever forget I love you, but also remember God loves you even more than I ever could. He remains your Heavenly Father no matter the circumstances of your life."

Scott also left messages for Lydia on separate tapes.

After four month, Scott had Lydia rig a remote control for the video camera. It had become harder for him to get out of his chair or the bed to change the camera settings.

Each week, Archie brought the Hospice workers by snowmobile. They met with the family several times to give encouragement and teach them how to deal with Scott's illness, aspects of his care, and involved Timmy.

They drew the couple apart for individual training and to meet their most pressing emotional needs.

That fourth month, Lydia was under stress and was late for her period. She carried hope in hear heart.

It was not to be.

I hate to tell Scott, he will feel another negative answer.

Lord, it is probably best, my body would have a hard time going through a pregnancy now with Scott so ill, but it is a disappointment. Timmy and I would have liked another reminder of Scott in our lives.

She didn't tell Scott until he asked.

He looked away. "I'm sorry. I would have liked to leave you another life and one of the things I know you wanted most. It would give you something to think about when I'm not around," Scott's voice broke.

"You know, God knows best. Timmy and I can manage, but I'd sure hate to go through delivery and the early days without you by my side. I'd be too helpless," she said.

Lydia turned her back and put Scott's socks into the dresser drawer.

Scott looked at her rigid spine. "You don't have to hold up for me all the time. Scream, yell, kick, cry, do whatever you need to, I can handle it," he whispered.

"I'm past some of that and I can't spend all my time crying. Timmy needs me and some semblance of routine and normal life," she said.

She turned and gathered Scott into her arms. He patted her back and soothed the ragged nerves they both had exposed. "I love you, Lydia. I pray God will meet all your needs . . . and keep you and Timmy safe and happy."

"I read in Psalms 36 about God's faithfulness. The Scriptures tell me, The clouds depend on Him. He makes fair decisions, He's firm like the mountains and deep like the sea. All of us and the animals are in His care. His love is a treasure to me. All find shelter under His wings," Scott added.

* * *

"Teach us to number our days." Scott read from Psalm 90. "Lydia, can I talk to you?"

Lydia sat on the side of their bed. *No, Lord, not now!*

Scott began, "We've got the paperwork done. I've talked to you and Archie about when I go. I'm very glad I took out the insurance policy with the forestry service and Equal-Life Company. That will provide you a monthly payment until Timmy is twenty-one or later, if he's still in college."

"Scott, I'm not sure I can deal with all this," she bowed her head so he wouldn't see the tears in her eyes. "It makes it sound like you've given up. I'm trying to hold on and not doing a very good job of it."

Scott reached for her and enclosed her in his once muscular arms.

"Lydia, I haven't given up, but outside a miracle, these are things we need to face. I don't think we can delay the inevitable. My physical situation is more untenable every time we go for treatment."

Scott continued, "I love you and wouldn't put you through this for anything. There's a lot of things out of my control now. No matter how hard we try, life is not going to continue as it has been. I've already surpassed what they first predicted. I'm not afraid to die, getting there is the hard part. I wish I could spare you and Timmy all of this," he talked fast in order to hold off raw emotions.

He looked down at Lydia, "If you need to get away, we could hire someone to come in and you could go visit your folks for a few days. I can not imagine what you are going through, no matter how I try."

She drew back and stared into his face. "Scott, I won't leave you. You're hurting my feelings to even mention it. I don't want to miss a moment of our life together." She broke down and sobbed into his flannel shirt.

Scott's tears flowed and mingled with hers.

When she got control, she raised her head. "Why does it have to be so hard? I hate to see you suffer, but I can't do much either. Scott, hold me."

"You do more than you think. You give me my medications, and hold me up with your prayers and presence. I love your strength and you, you're all I've ever wanted for a partner," he said. "Now, you need to take care of yourself and Timmy. God will be with us all."

"Lydia, I've made lists of our savings and investments we've made over the years. You'll find all the paper work in our roll-top desk in our lock box. If you need to, you can cash in some of the bonds, otherwise, use it for Timmy's education." He looked around, "You can sell the cabin if you need to."

Lydia shook her head, "I don't ever want to sell the cabin. We need to be here. It's our home. Someday, I will probably go back to work, but we won't sell it."

"I am glad you'll keep the cabin. I love it here and I

know you both do too," he said. "We put a lot of ourselves into our home."

Lydia looked at his drawn face, "Scott, you need your pills, don't you?"

"Yes, I've held off about as long as I can," he scrunched down lower in bed.

She took the key from atop the safe door facing, opened their roll-top desk, and reached for the pain medication in the third row of pills. *So many, so very many, and not a one really helps.*

She poured the tablets into her hand, got a glass of water from the kitchen sink and carried all to Scott, along with a soda cracker. He ate the cracker to cushion the impact on his stomach, downed the pills and lay back.

"Don't forget, I love you," he sighed and closed is eyes.

"Always," she replied.

"Always," Scott returned.

He prayed silently the thoughts from Psalms 80:19. *'Lord God, you are all powerful. Make us strong again. Smile on us and save us,' but how? I can't shout and be happy about leaving Lydia and Timmy. Help me to be happy, no matter my state.*

You numbered my days from the beginning of time. You knew how long I'd have. I thank and praise You for that time. I pray the days were well-spent. Please forgive me for those that were not used well.

Bless Timmy and Lydia all the days of their lives and take us all home when our days on earth are spent.

Thank You.

Lingering

Scott became desperate to tell his family all that he wished to before his time came.

"Lydia, I lived my dream. I got to come to my mountain and I got to marry you, and we had Timmy. I had my life dream and I'm grateful to God and to you for loving me." He buried his face in her neck for a long time.

Lydia thought she felt a tear trickle from his cheek.

"I feel good about fathering Timmy. You won't be alone. He's someone for you to love. I helped protect God's creation. I pray I did enough in telling and showing others about God," he murmured.

He was quiet for a moment and started again, "You know the country western song, 'If tomorrow never comes, did I tell you that I loved you?' Did I tell you enough? I'm sorry for times I let you down or got busy with my own things. I needed to tell you more times how special you are and how much I love you. I don't have regrets, I want you and Timmy to live long and happy lives, then one day, we'll meet again when we all gather in heaven."

When Timmy was near his father, he played on the rug or took naps beside his Daddy. Sometimes he put his animals on the blankets and talked about them. Scott added a few comments, but mostly his stamina was so low, he watched his son. Pride and pain showed on his face. Sometimes Lydia saw a tear. A couple of times, Timmy crawled up to hug his father and lay his cheek on his Daddy's.

Such a caring little fellow. I wish Scott could get up and go run up the trails. I wish Timmy could go to the mountain with his Daddy again. I wish they could swim and dive again.

She turned away, fearful Scott would see her emotion on her face.

Scott pondered Psalms 88 and the people's prayer when they thought they would soon be dead. He anguished as they had.

He felt compelled to give Lydia information, he felt she might need, or that he wanted her to know, thinking it might also help her at some time.

"I ignored some messages from my body," Scott said.

Lydia was stricken. "I didn't know you had symptoms, why didn't you tell me?"

"It wasn't any big thing. I thought I was just tired. We work hard in the spring and summer. We are always a little worn-down that time of year. I usually revive during hunting season. I thought that was all, or even getting older. It wasn't anything big, just a few little things, but I should have been wise enough to have it checked out," he said.

"I think I knew you weren't quite up to par last spring. I should have said something to you," Lydia said. "And you were coughing too."

"For not seeking medical help, I am responsible and no one else really knew. I've accepted that responsibility and my mistakes. God knew what I was going to do and my faults. I've wasted some of my life in a way, but perhaps He will allow me to minister even in my illness and death."

Lydia turned and looked out the window. She could not let Scott look into her eyes at this moment.

Scott continued, "I have two buddies I need to talk with. I want to use my voice and body to the last minute to honor God, like it says in I Corinthians 6:10."

Scott also studied Psalm 19:1.

By this time, Timmy was beginning to understand that something was terribly wrong. His Daddy wasn't well.

Scott was no longer able to play with the boy in the

way that the two had played. They had wrestled, ran up the trails, or Scott carried the boy on his shoulders. They had dived and swam together, with Scott taking the child on his back or pulling him through the water. No longer could Scott do anything, other than sit quietly and watch Timmy as the little boy played alone.

Timmy became frustrated and acted out. Sometimes he ran to his room and slammed the door.

Scott saw his little boy with tears in his eyes.

"What's the matter, Buddy?" he asked.

"I'm mad at God. He lets you be sick and I don't want Him to do that," Timmy said, then jumped into his Daddy's arms.

"Buddy, you know we don't have to like what happens, but we need to remember this, God loved us so much He sent His Son to die on the cross for us so all we have to do is to believe in Him, and ask Him into our hearts so He can live with us. He'll be with us all the time, no matter what happens to us. We can cry, but sometimes, we just have to be tough and take it, whatever that happens to be. Come here, Son."

Timmy climbed onto his father's lap. Scott gathered his son closer and hugged the little body to himself.

They were so quiet, Timmy drifted off to sleep.

Scott relished the feel of life in his son. He could feel the beat of the little heart within the boy's ribs, the rise and fall of the small chest.

Scott bowed his head and prayed for all the times he wouldn't be here to comfort and love his child.

He lay his face against the smaller head. He smelled the little boy smell with a vague scent of soap, shampoo, and little boy sweat.

So hard to leave, so hard. Lord, help me.

By the end of several months, Scott weakened to the point he could only talk for a few minutes at a time. He saved these precious moments for messages of love.

He often lay in one of the chairs on the deck and watched the mountain and the animals that came and went.

Timmy quietly played in the sand or talked to his father. Every time his Daddy didn't answer, Timmy continued to talk of anything he could think of to delay losing his father.

Scott would smile when Timmy looked at him.

Lydia sat by Scott's side when she had necessities cared for.

They stayed outside on the deck, especially in the evenings.

Neighbors came and prayed. They brought food. Some didn't want to see Scott. Personal mortality came closer. It preyed on everyone's mind.

Scott's parents came for frequent visits. After a couple of days, Scott was able to tell his parents, "Mom and Dad. . . You need to go home to your work."

"We want to be here for you, Son."

"I know. . . I need peace and rest. We're doing okay. It's not good for you and Dad . . . to be here. I don't want to hurt you. . . I love you. . . go home, please, Mom," Scott begged.

"Help me, Mom. . . I don't have energy to help Dad . . . now. All I can do is love you both. . . I can't deal with anything else."

Scott's mother visited with Vera. "He's worried about us. That keeps him from resting as he should."

"Maybe you should follow his wishes and go home. Then come back for short times," Vera advised.

His parents left with great reluctance. They tried to be

stoic as they hugged the family and told them they'd be back soon.

"We love you, Scott. Lydia, take care of yourself and Timmy. We'll be back if you need us. Call anytime," they turned to leave. Both felt they might not see their son alive again.

When they got beyond the bend, Scott's father pulled the car over to the edge of the road.

They collapsed into each other's arms and cried out in their grief.

The little family continued to tie up loose ends and prepare for the time Scott would be gone.

He looked at Lydia, "How could Jesus get everything done . . . in thirty-three years? I'm thirty and had a lot of work yet to do. . .Martin Luther King Junior said. . . 'I have a dream.' He didn't finish his. . .I'm not going to finish mine. Our dreams were too big for one man." He smiled. "God's going. . . to do this one too."

"Scott, God made these mountains many, many years ago. He's had a lot of people working and He'll provide others to pick up the baton. You can talk to your colleagues. Some of your dream is also theirs. If God wants it done, He'll do it," Lydia said.

"I loved my work. . . I think I made a difference. There's a couple of guys . . . I need to talk to. . . I've written e-mails. . . they will probably be here tomorrow. . . the next day. . . They both need Jesus. . . Pray for them, and me. . . I can get the message. . . across to them," Scott pleaded.

Scott indicated that when his friends came, he wished to talk to them and then if they weren't ready, he wanted Lydia to go through the Roman Road method of telling them about Christ and His salvation.

"I'll buzz. . . the phone button. . . you come," Scott said.

After her study that evening, Lydia marked the proper passages in a couple of New Testaments and laid the two books on the dining room table.

When Scott's two friends came, she welcomed them into their home.

Drew and Sam each gave her a quick hug.

"How's he doing?" Drew asked.

"I'm glad you fellows could come. Scott has been wanting to see you for a month, but there just didn't seem to be a good time. He's in the bedroom and wants you to come right on in," she said.

"Is he well enough to see us?" Sam asked.

"We can do it another time, if he's not up to it," Drew said.

Lydia looked at the two. "I'll be frank, he's not well, but he really needs to see you guys. Talking to you has been heavy on his mind. If he doesn't get the opportunity, he won't rest."

She led them into the bedroom for their visit with Scott.

Shocked at Scott's condition, both tried to hide their discomfort.

"Are you up to seeing us today? We could come back another time if you're not," Sam said.

Drew moved his hat around in his hand and after an initial view, looked away, uncomfortable with his friend's condition.

"I need to tell you. . . something. Have a . . . seat," Scott said.

Lydia returned to the dining room. With her head

bowed and the phone near her hand, she opened one of the marked New Testaments she had in readiness. She prayed for Drew's and Sam's salvation, and for Scott to have the words and strength to give his friends the message he desired to offer.

She could hear the murmur of voices from the bedroom, but couldn't tell what was said. Scott's voice was so low, she was unable to hear him speak.

When Scott began to tell his friends why he'd contacted them. Drew became stiff and sat down away from Scott's bed.

Sam seated himself in the chair beside the head of Scott's bed.

"That is something I've thought about a lot," he said.

"You're. . . good men. . . but that's. . . not enough. You have to . . . believe in Jesus. . . as the Son. . . of God... and ask Him to. . . save you."

Sam had a tear on his cheek. "If you believe and say that's the thing to do, I'm ready, Buddy. Tell me how."

Scott took a couple of breaths. "Say something like this. . . I know I have sinned. . . forgive me. . . I believe Jesus is. . . God's Son. . .I want Him. . . in my heart. . . Save me."

Sam whispered the words with his eyes closed.

The room was very quiet for several moments.

Sam raised his head with a glow to his face.

"I did it and I've already got a weight off my shoulders. I wanted to ask you a lot of times, but somehow it never came up. Thank you, Buddy." He clasped Scott's hand, then was overcome and reached to give his friend a hug.

Scott hugged back with tears on his cheeks too.

Drew looked on but was not convinced.

Scott was emotional and struggled to take deep breathes and regain his strength.

"Read the book. . . of John. . .and the Gospels. Lydia

will . . . show you. She has. . . a marked. . . New Testament
. . .to give you. . .Find a church. . . let the minister. . .
someone help you," Scott was wearing out quickly but he
looked at Drew and felt the burden return to minister to his
other good friend.

"Can Lydia come in. . . and read from the Bible?"
Scott asked.

Drew nodded. *I love this guy, but he's in this shape
and believes God is with him? How, when he's dying? If he
wants to talk or have Lydia talk, I'd do anything for him, so
let it happen.*

Scott punched the telephone button.

Lydia jumped, she'd been so deeply into prayer, she
was startled. She got up from the table and hurried into their
bedroom.

"Hi, you fellows need something?" she asked.

Scott motioned with his hand, "Read . . . for Drew."

Lydia noted that both Scott and Sam bowed their
heads and closed their eyes. That gave her strength to plunge
in.

"Drew, I have this marked New Testament for you.
Let me go through a few things with you and then you can
take it with you so that you can read it again for yourself."

Lydia began to read from John 3:16. "Then go to
Romans 3:23; Romans 5:8; and John 1:2."

She allowed the markings with the next page number
to lead her to the next designated page. "I've marked in the
front cover the first verse, then the page number and high
lighted the verse on the designated page. You can look over
it again on your own. If you don't understand, come back or
ask a Christian friend or minister. Vera and Archie will help
you anytime."

After she read several verses, Drew held his palm
toward Lydia, "Whoa, whoa, you're giving me more than I

can digest. What's this about sin? I'm a good person, I don't steal, cheat on my wife, drink or gamble."

Scott raised his head from the pillow. "You are a good guy. . .but you must. . . be perfect."

"Well, I'm not perfect, no one is. There's a few little things I do," Drew said.

"That's it. . . none are perfect. . . Jesus took. . . .our sins. . . Lydia." Scott said.

She reread where the Bible stated that none was perfect, no not one, other than Jesus.

"It's that simple. You surrender and God does the work. Jesus already gave his life to take care of your sin. All you have to do is believe and ask him and he'll save you," she repeated.

"Scott, and Lydia, I won't lie to you. I don't understand, but I promise you, I will read the book Lydia gave me and I will think about it. That's all I can do for now. I do admire what you have. What Lydia has, but. . I just don't know, it's a big step and I want to talk to my wife about it," Drew said.

He shook Scott's hand and clasped his shoulder. "We better go and let you rest. You look tuckered. We'll be back. Don't give up," he turned way.

Sam gave his friend another hug. He spoke, "You gave me the most wonderful gift I've ever received. Thank you, Man."

Scott smiled, "Thank you. I'll pray. . . for you." He looked past Sam. "Drew? . . . You too."

"Thanks," Drew stepped to the bedroom door and Sam followed.

Sam looked back at Scott and flashed him a thumbs up signal. "Be seeing you. I'll pray too."

"Do that," Scott replied.

Lydia went to Scott. She adjusted his pillow and

hugged him. "We'll all be praying. One down and the other one thinking, and Drew promised to read the Bible I think he's serious. He'll get there yet."

Scott closed is eyes and let out a big breath.

"Do you need your pills?" Lydia asked.

"Good. . . idea," he murmured.

*   *   *

"Lydia, about all . . . I've got left is my spirit. I love you with . . . all my heart. . . Thank you for loving me . . . giving good advice. . . I need you to ground me."

"This isn't happening. . . just to me. You and Timmy . . . experiencing it too. . . hardest part, I don't want you . . . both to suffer," Scott said.

Lydia had no answer to all the questions that arose. The best she could do was console Scott or change the subject.

She went down to visit Vera while Archie was with Scott.

Later in the week, Lydia set up her easel in their room so she could be near Scott to meet his needs. She needed to occupy her hands; contain her emotions; and painting would not disturb Scott's rest. She used water colors to prevent any odor that might hamper his breathing.

As she painted, her mind roamed. She thought of Pope Paul VI's quote: *'Whatever you want to do, do it now! There are only so many tomorrows.'* She looked at her husband as he lay propped high on pillows. *'God never wastes what he creates.' Where did I read that?*

She set her paint brush in the water can and crawled to Scott's side. Her arm crept around his wasted body.

"Lydia?" Scott whispered.

"I'm here. I thought you were asleep?" she said.

"Thinking. . . I want to die well. . ." he said.

"Don't worry about that," she scolded, her heart pierced.

"God is bigger than. . . this cancer. He'll take me home. . . and cancer will be . . . defeated. . .Again."

"Yes, Scott, God will defeat this cancer, one way or another," she agreed.

All was quiet. Scott's breathing evened-out and he appeared to rest.

He then spoke again, " 'Solomon in all his glory was not . . . arrayed like these. . .Grass withers and is gone'. . . as human bodies. . . are gone. . . from the earth. . .I surrender. God, can do with me . . . what He will. . ."

He was quiet for a time. "I never expected. . . our parents to experience. . . some of the things. . . they have. . . this included."

"Life is more. . . than I've known. . . thus far. I'm ready to go . . . to the next level . . . but I groan and ache for you . . . for Timmy. . . our parents," Scott murmured.

The doctors suggested a feeding tube. Scott was vehement, "It has been painful. . . to get to this point. . . I don't want to . . . prolong my life unnaturally."

When they arrived back home, Lydia worried about his lack of appetite.

Scott said, "Graham cracker. . . don't worry. . . what I eat."

Lydia laid her finger on his lips, "Just know we want you with us. You can't stay if you don't eat," Lydia said. She looked at his face. "I won't say anymore, but if you think of something you want, please tell us."

By this time, Scott could hardly be moved in a wheel chair.

By fall, the medical personnel implanted a morphine

pump for Scott to administer his own pain medication when his pain became intense. The home health care workers came by to refill the pump and take care of the more difficult procedures. They brought a lift to help Lydia move Scott in and out of bed, and his chair.

Several times, Lydia came upon Scott as he pored over the book of Job.

He spoke to her softly. "Whatever happens. . . keep your faith in God."

* * *

No longer could he get out of bed. Lydia propped him with pillows on his side or raised his head. She bathed him several times a day and Timmy lay beside him on the pillow.

Lydia agonized, *I can see cancer draining the life from his body, hour by hour. I can't stand it! This insidious monster! I wish there was someway to attack it and bring it to defeat. So many suffer, so many. Their families too.*

One evening, Scott was very quiet. Finally, Lydia asked, "Scott, is there something on your mind?"

"Yes," his speech was hesitant. He stopped between words for breath. "Philippians 3: . .13."

Lydia reached for their bedside Bible and turned to the chapter and verse. She glanced at it and choked.

"Read," Scott whispered.

"Forgetting those things which are behind and reaching forward to those things which are ahead. . .," she could read no more. In a moment, she asked, "What?"

Scott took a big breath, "You, Tim,. . . go on. . . live, don't look back." He exhaled and labored for the next breath. "Be happy . . . find peace . . . joy. . . Don't be sad for. . . too long."

Lydia fell on her knees and buried her face in Scott's shoulder.

Slowly his hand rose and he lay it on her head.

Lydia realized his hand felt heavy. *He can't hold it up himself anymore.* She reached up and clasped his fingers, gathered her strength and rose.

"We'll be okay, God will see us through," she said.

Scott looked into her face. His love shown, "My blessing . . . upon. . . whatever. . . you decide," he breathed.

Lydia reached down and hugged him around his shoulders. *So thin, so very thin. I can feel his bones. He's like fluff about to blow away. Oh, God, don't let him blow away from us!*

Scott saw her tears track down her cheeks. His fell too.

"Mommy, are you here? Where's Daddy?" Timmy called from the stairs to his mother.

Lydia wiped her cheek quickly with the back of her hand. She ran a thumb down each of Scott's cheeks and turned to the door, "We're here, Son, in the bedroom."

Going Home

The hunting season was well-advanced. Scott had realized months ago, he'd never hunt again.

Lydia had their bed turned so he faced the window and could look up the mountain.

Scott, Lydia, and Timmy watched the hunters come down the mountain with their meat, hides and trophies.

Scott's friends stopped by occasionally to give him reports, but his world narrowed with each day.

Scott's last day, Lydia and Timmy lay down beside him, one on either side.

His breathing grew more ragged as the day progressed. Lydia felt he would soon go. *Oh, Lord, I don't want him to go, but I can't stand for him to suffer.*

Lydia and Timmy talked to him all day of their love but finally Lydia said, "I don't want to jar or hurt you."

Later, his hand crept to hers.

"Scott, we love you more than we can say, I don't know how to say this. We know how bad you hurt. We'll let you go be with Jesus whenever you need to. You do what you have to and we'll understand. We love you."

He breathed a sigh. "Thanks." Scott moved his eyes to look at her and moved his lips in a silent, "I love you."

Timmy raised up to look into his Daddy's face.

"I love you, Daddy."

Scott mouthed, "Me too," and closed his eyes, totally exhausted. He pressed his morphine pump and drifted off into drugged sleep. Three times in the night, he signaled for Lydia to press the pump as his breathing became more and more labored and hesitant.

Lydia and Timmy hugged his body, their arms stretched across and joined to each other.

Several times in the night, Timmy drifted off to sleep for a time.

Lydia prayed, sometimes aloud. She hoped Scott could hear. Sometimes she poured out her heart to God. She hoped Scott would not hear as she anguished.

At dawn, Scott opened his eyes.

Lydia looked at him. *The spark of life is leaving his eyes. He's going. Oh, God, don't do this to him and us!*

He rattled a breath. His hand brushed Lydia's and Timmy's. His family raised up to look more fully into his face. He gazed first at Timmy, then Lydia, closed his eyes and stopped breathing.

All was quiet for a few seconds.

"Daddy?" Timmy cried.

Lydia let out a breath, "Honey, he's gone to be with Jesus. He doesn't hurt anymore," she whispered.

"I'm glad, but Mommy, I want my Daddy," he whimpered.

"I know, Honey, but there's not a thing we can do about it. We'll see him again in Heaven, until then, we have to do the best we can. We've got each other and we'll make it. Daddy wanted us to be strong for each other. You and me, Buddy," Lydia whispered. She gave him a strong squeeze.

Lydia buried her face in Scott's shoulder and Timmy covered his face with his free hand. They lay thus for a short time.

Lydia had shed so many tears in the last months, she had none at the moment. Those would come later, at night, when Timmy wasn't present.

"Mommy, I gotta go," Timmy said.

"Okay, Son, can you go by yourself?" she knew he didn't want to leave his father or her.

"Uh-huh," he climbed off the bed and headed past the window.

"Mommy, look, there's an *humongous* elk standing in the yard!"

As they watched the bull looked at them through the window, bowed his head, then turned and went back up the mountain. He stopped broadside to them in an opening amongst the fir trees, then turned and disappeared into the mist.

"Do you think that was God coming after Daddy?" Timmy whispered.

"He could have been a messenger from God telling us Daddy was okay and with Jesus," Lydia replied.

"It makes me feel better if Daddy went with the big elk," the boy said.

"Me too, Buddy."

When Lydia thought Archie and Vera would be awake, she spoke to Timmy, "I need to call Archie. Scott told him what he wanted us to do when he went with Jesus, so I have to let Archie know. I'm going to bathe your Daddy, then we'll wrap him up in the blanket with the big elk pictures on it. He'd like that. Archie will come and they will take his old body away. Your Daddy already has a new strong body in heaven. He doesn't need this one and he doesn't hurt anymore."

"What are they going to do with Daddy?" Timmy asked.

"They will bring back his ashes and we'll take them up the mountain to that spot you and he liked where the trails meet. We'll sprinkle his ashes there. The Forestry Service is going to send some of his old friends and they'll put up a marker for him."

* * *

The church held a service of remembrances. Then the details occurred exactly as Lydia had explained to Timmy.

The crewmen from the Forestry Service arrived with the bronze plaque to attach to the face of the cliff above Scott's favorite spot. Drew and Sam were two of the crew.

Timmy, Lydia, Archie, Vera, and the four men went up the mountain together. They walked through the snow. Timmy carried the *treasure chest* with his Daddy's ashes. Lydia walked beside him.

"Mommy, I'm carrying Daddy. I never could do that before," Timmy said.

"He's lighter now, God is carrying your Daddy for you," she murmured.

He's such a little man. He's far too young to be going through this kind of thing, I wish we could have spared him all this.

Everyone was quiet as they advanced to the cliff. The men hammered bronze spikes through the holes in the plaque.

Lydia read the message to Timmy. "Scott's Mountain, Scott Timothy Thayer, October 26, 2002. 'I will lift up mine eyes unto the hills from whence cometh my help. My help comes from the Lord, the Maker of heaven and earth. Psalms 121.'"

Sam came to put his arm around Lydia and his hand on Timmy's head.

Drew tucked his head and faced Lydia.

"I did it, I asked Jesus into my heart. My wife did too. I didn't get to tell Scott, but somehow I think he knows," his voice broke.

Tears welled in Lydia's eyes, "We're so glad and the angels in heaven rejoice. Scott is amongst them, I think he knows too."

The three friends enclosed the little boy in their midst and bowed their heads in prayer.

Lydia closed, "Thank you, Lord."

Vera and Archie heard and came to enfold the four friends.

The other two crewmen turned and started down the mountain with their equipment. They were baffled by the happenings.

Sam said, "We will make certain our co-workers understand our newfound salvation. Scott showed us how and his example will grow."

"God bless you both and we'll be praying for the guys," Lydia said.

She turned to her son. "Timmy, guess we'd better go before it gets too cold out here. It looks like it could snow again. We'd better get home before then."

"What about Daddy?" he asked.

"He's not here, he's with God. It is perfect there, he won't be cold or sick, or sad ever again. We have to be happy for Daddy," she said.

"But can I be sad?" Timmy asked.

Drew and Sam each took hold and hoisted him between them. Each man had their arms under him for support in a two-fireman's carry.

"We can be sad, but Scott rests in the arms of Jesus tonight and that's the most wonderful place anywhere," Drew added. "I'm sure God knows how to carry a man even better than we do."

"Yeah, we know how to carry a man, but not as good as God does," Sam said.

Timmy chuckled as the men bounced him along the trail. Lydia watched.

"Thank you, Lord, for good friends and men. Timmy needs that now."

The two men started with long strides down the mountain.

Lydia followed more sedately.

She turned back for one last look before she ran after them.

*   *   *

At first, Lydia was unable to look at Scott's videos. She had copies made and on her next trip to town, she rented a safe deposit box at the bank. She placed Scott's original tapes inside for safe keeping.

Scott had organized and made a list of each date, or topic he had felt Timmy or Lydia might need.

She had alphabetized the list and placed a copy in their lock box at the cabin. The videos, she filed in the bookcase at home.

She ran her finger down the backs of the cases where the titles marched along side by side.

Scott worked so hard on these. Someday, I will be able to look at them. I can't right now.

Months Later

Lydia and Timmy mourned the death of their husband and father in the best way they could. When the burden became too heavy, they went to see the pastor or visited with Archie and Vera. Timmy would soon go outside to work with Archie and Lydia unloaded to Vera.

Having been through the death of her first husband, Vera offered sound advice and counsel.

Vera rocked Lydia as the younger woman cried or talked. Vera mothered Lydia, as Lydia did for Timmy most nights in Daddy's big chair.

"Does Timmy ever cry?" Vera asked.

"Yes, he does cry occasionally, but children seem to be able to cry one minute and play the next. He misses his Daddy, but I try to keep him very busy. We talk about Scott, but I try to make certain most of the memories are pleasant. His greatest fear is that one of the hunters will kill the big bull elk that came after Scott's death," Lydia said. "I don't know what he'll do if one of the hunters carries that carcass by our house."

"You could go away for a few days until the hunters clear out for the winter," Vera suggested, "but as far as the elk being gone from the mountain, I wouldn't cross that bridge until I came to it. God will give you the right words."

Vera continued, "It will get easier with time. You will keep being more and more able to remember the good times and put the difficulties of Scott's death behind you. I know that sounds unbelievable to you, but I think you will find it to be true. I think Timmy is doing well."

"He isn't really. He has nightmares. I spend most nights on his floor beside his bed. I might as well move another bed into his room and sleep there," Lydia sighed.

"Would that be so bad? I think you both need each other now. He'll be okay one of these days. He needs something to take his mind off his loss. Have you thought about going back to the city and letting him enter school so he'd have more friends his own age?" Vera asked.

"I am thinking about it, but I'm also having a very hard time thinking of leaving our home or. . . Scott's Mountain." Lydia had tears in her eyes.

*   *   *

Neither of them wanted to leave their mountain. They didn't manage to get away that school year. Lydia felt there were more important tasks for them at home.

The next fall, after the death of his father, Timmy ran screaming into the house, "Mommy, the hunters are coming. They're driving up the mountain!"

"I know. It's that time of year. Don't you remember your Daddy always went up the mountain when the aspens turned golden and red?"

"Yes, but Mommy, they'll hurt Daddy."

"Don't you know, he's in heaven with Jesus? They can't hurt Daddy."

"But, when Daddy died, I thought he went with the big bull?" Timmy said.

"God could send us a sign, my big boy. God could send any thing he wanted to make us feel better. If the elk was an angel, it took Daddy on to heaven. If the elk wasn't an angel, God took Scott. Daddy isn't out in the mountains anymore, he's in heaven," Lydia explained.

"How do you know they aren't out on the mountains?" he asked.

"God made everything and He could send whatever He wanted to us. He could send an Angel as an elk, or He might have sent us the big bull just to make us feel better, we don't have to know. We know Daddy's already with God. Jesus said on the cross when He was talking with one of the thieves, 'Today you'll be with me in Paradise.'"

"Okay," Tim agreed.

But his mind was not at peace. Each day, Timmy watched every truck or ATV as it came down the mountain to have the harvest checked through the weigh station. Each day he grew more and more nervous when the trucks came into sight. Lydia watched and worried that her son was so distraught by the presence of the hunters, she considered going to her parents' home for a visit. Somehow she knew being away would worry Timmy even more.

Her only solution seemed to be extra hugs. She slept in the sleeping bag by his bed to awaken him from his frequent nightmares. Part of each night, she wrapped them both in a fleecy blanket and rocked him in the big chair Scott had given her for her birthday before Timmy was born. Scott had said it was for the baby.

Previously, many hours had been spent there during

fevers and teething, but now the chair served a larger purpose. While Lydia rocked or held Timmy, she spent the quiet hours thinking of their life while Scott lived.

Several mornings she and Timmy looked at the videos of their family life during happier times.

On several occasions, Timmy asked his mother to put on the tape Scott had made for his first birthday without his Daddy. For her, it opened wounds, but Timmy seemed to take joy in the pictures and words of his father.

She reminisced about their early married years, then on into Timmy's birth and their joy. Then she dwelt on Scott's diagnosis, his illness and his death in her arms with Timmy holding his Daddy's hand.

Every few days during the remainder of the hunting season, some of the pack llamas came down with elk quarters or racks packed aboard, but never the big antlers from the massive bull.

Finally the snow flew and the mountainside was blocked out. The hunting season ended on the same day.

The next morning, the clouds cleared and Timmy awoke to a glistening world of serene white. He looked out his upstairs window and his eyes were nearly blinded by the brilliance. He squinted at the dark shape coming from the tree line. He looked again.

"Mommy, look!" He scampered down the stairs to take his mother's hand. He drew her to the big window where Daddy had captured the view of the mountainside when they built their log home.

"Look. Look, there's the big bull. He made it through the season. Do you think God sent him back to show me he was still okay?" Timmy asked.

"God could do that. He knew you were very worried and He loves us. He wouldn't want you to keep worrying," Lydia said.

"Look, Mom, he's coming into the yard. He's almost to the window. I've never seen an elk get so close. Does he want something?" Timmy asked.

"I don't know, but maybe we could throw out a carrot. He'd probably like that, but we can't go out on the lawn. This time of year, the bulls can be dangerous," Lydia cautioned.

"But if God sent him, he won't be. He's here to tell us Daddy is okay." Tim's voice showed his conviction.

"God doesn't want us to be careless. I'll step out on the deck and drop the carrot in front of him. You stay right inside the window and watch to see what he does. Usually I can't open the door without them spooking, so stay very quiet," Lydia directed.

She got several carrots from the refrigerator and eased the deck door open. She crept to the railing, slowly raised her arm and tossed a carrot underhanded. The elk watched but didn't flinch as the carrot landed between his front hooves. He looked into her eyes, then shifted to look at Timmy through the glass. He bowed his head, then reached to retrieve the carrot. He lifted his left hoof to paw the offering out of the snow. He raised his head with one end of the carrot sticking from the corner of his mouth. Several strong crunches and the carrot disappeared. She threw another carrot, but the elk bowed his head again, then strolled back toward the timber.

Timmy stepped to the deck and yelled. "Bye, Daddy."

The big bull looked back over his shoulder and lifted his massive antlers high. He trotted broadside and disappeared into the dark evergreens.

In a moment, Lydia and Timmy saw him in a bare spot. The bull turned on the hillside and looked back toward them, then he faded away.

Tears silently rivered down Lydia's face and dripped into the snow on the railing.

"Thank you God for the comfort you've given both of us. Keep your creatures safe this winter," she prayed aloud.

Timmy took his mother's hand and looked into her face.

"Amen," the little boy said.

They were both quiet through the lunch hour.

After they cleared up the dishes, he took her hand and led her to the hearth.

"Tell me a Daddy story, about when he was my age."

"I don't know everything, because I didn't know Daddy at that time. He liked to go in a canoe with his Daddy. You know his Daddy was your Pawpaw Thayer?"

"I know that. Daddy told me a long time ago," he replied.

"I was sure he did, but I thought I'd remind you," Lydia said. She tousled his already messy head of dark curls. "Your other grandma and grandpa are my parents and Aunt Susie is my sister. Susie's kids are your cousins. Your Daddy didn't have any brothers or sisters."

*   *   *

Timmy got his father's camouflage cap from the coat closet.

"Mommy, can I have this?" he asked.

Lydia looked. It's a little big yet. You could wait a couple of years, then it would fit."

Timmy looked at her. His eyes welled.

She hugged him to her, "Sure, you can have it. Do you want me to try to stitch it up for you?"

His face took on a panicked look. "No, I don't want to wear it!"

"It's fine for you to have it, but what are you going to

do with it, if you're not going to wear it?" she asked.

"I'm going to smell it. It smells like Daddy." He clapped the cap over his face. His voice was muffled.

Lydia turned away to keep Timmy from seeing her own tears.

Winter Passed and Spring Advanced

Lydia spent some of her sleepless nights creating God's Messenger for Timmy's wall quilt.

She worked on a frame for the quilt with tie-dyed and painted strips of cloth. On the bottom, she embroidered. "I will lift up my eyes into the hills, from whence comes my help."

She hung it back on the wall while Timmy was with Archie. They didn't turn on his lights when he went up to bed that evening.

When he awakened, he looked up.

"Mommy, you got it finished! I like the old bull. He's always on my wall now. It looks like clouds on the side and the top," he said.

"Think of it as *The Heavens*," Lydia said.

A few days later, Lydia finally informed her son of recent developments and decisions that must be made.

"Timmy, I think we'd better plan to go into town this next winter. We need to find me a job and you can go to school and have more friends," Lydia told the growing boy. "I've checked out a teaching position at Gunnison, they've accepted my credentials and sent a contract. I need to sign that and get it back to them very soon. In fact, I need to call them with my answer and the contract will go out when we go down to see Archie and Vera today."

She talked, to convince both of them.

Timmy looked around the cabin.

She hurried to assure him.

"We'll keep the cabin. We can come home on long weekends, Thanksgiving, Christmas, and we'll spend the summers here. Archie and Vera said they'd take care of it for us when we're gone."

"Mommy, I don't want to leave Daddy," Timmy whimpered.

"We won't be leaving Daddy. He's as near us in town as he is here. I know you love it here and so do I, but we need to be with people and I need to work again. It will be good for both of us and then we'll come back here every chance we get. It won't be easy at first, but we really need to do this. I hope you can be a little bit happy about a new adventure."

"You've never lived in town, but there are a lot of things to do. We could have pizza at the pizza shop any time we wanted. We could go to movies in a theater. We could go to the zoo and see all the animals. We could go to an ice skating rink and learn to skate. There are many other things but I can't tell you all we could find to do. You'd have a lot of friends at your new school," Lydia tried to convince her son as much as she tried to convince herself.

City Life

Archie came to assist them in winterizing the cabin.

Lydia was to teach art in two of the elementary schools in Gunnison, Colorado, that fall.

They moved to a small house within walking distance of their schools. Timmy was to attend the primary school where Lydia taught art on two days a week. She was to spend the other days at the older children's school.

Routine settled in for them. They still missed Scott, but both kept very busy.

Out of a blue day, Timmy asked, "Will I ever have brothers or sisters?"

An arrow speared her heart. "God will have to tell us that and He hasn't yet. Your Dad and I wanted a big family. Daddy didn't want you to be an only child like he was. He said it was too lonely to be the only kid." She tickled his ribs, "But then again, sometimes it was nice, because he got all the presents and all his parents' time."

She continued, "Probably if they'd had a raft of kids, they couldn't have taken him to so many places and he wouldn't have seen so many things."

"They might not have had enough money, or the car might not have been big enough, or. . ."

"Oh, Mommy, you're kidding me. They could have gotten a van, like my friend Greg. He has five kids in his family and they all have seats in their minivan, even with a few left over. You know I've gone with them to soccer games and we went with them to the zoo that one time. There was even a seat for you too."

"Yes, that's right. Did you know there weren't minivans when I was a little girl. Mostly people got station wagons if they needed bigger cars," Lydia said.

"What's a station wagon?" he asked.

"It's like your friend Molly's mom drives. The back is kind of square and instead of a trunk, there's an extra seat back toward the square part," she explained.

"Yeah, I rode on that preschool Sunday School field trip in a station wagon. It was cool. I wish we had one of those, I could even put the seat down and sleep in it. Could we get a station wagon or a minivan?" he asked.

"I don't think so. Our family isn't big enough. You and I just need a seat each," Lydia said. "Our car uses less gas too. We need to watch that. Daddy worked to save our environment and we need to do that too."

"We might get more kids, or a Daddy, then we'd need a bigger car," Timmy added.

"Well, let's not get a bigger car until we need it. The car we have now is just right for us, I can even lay down the back seat and push our long things through from the trunk. Do you remember when I brought home the basketball goal in the back with the seat down?" she asked.

"Yeah, I was at school and you got it for my birthday. When I got home, it was set up on the driveway. We played a game when I got home that evening. Can I take my goal with us to the mountain this summer?" Timmy asked.

"You need to sit in the back seat, so I'd have to fold down the other half. We might be able to get it and all our luggage into the car on the other side, if we can pile it on top of the goal. We'll give it a try and see how it works when we go," Mom said. "We couldn't pile it on top of you though. You've got to have your seat clear and our packing needs to be safe for us all."

"Don't you want your goal here in the spring?" Lydia asked.

"It won't be warm enough for long. If we wait till summer, we won't have room to take it," Timmy said. "We could take it when we go Christmas and leave it there for this summer. It's in the garage, I can't play basketball in the snow now, so I don't need it on the driveway."

"That's an idea. You're smart like your Daddy. We won't take as much when we go in the winter, so we probably could fit it in with one of the seats down. We'd need to tie it down, I wouldn't want that pole bouncing around if we had to stop fast. We'll give it a try," she said.

Daddy Stories

"Tell me another Daddy story," became Tim's mantra each evening when she tucked him into bed.

During the day, she dredged up some painful memories to compose in a way her son could cherish them as she did. She felt it was good for him to talk of his father and she didn't want him to forget his daddy, but she didn't want to make him sad near bedtime. She had enough trouble with night time and didn't want to add his crying during the night, to her own loneliness.

Some of the most dreadful nights, she arose and painted the night away. One night, she painted their family from the photo that sat on the mantel. It turned out well and Timmy was excited about the new, larger version of their picture.

"Mommy, can we get a frame and hang it above the fireplace in our cabin? That way we could sit and look at the picture when we're in front of our big fireplace," he commented.

"That's the best idea you've had today. Let's do it. What color frame do you want?" she asked.

"Maybe orange," he said.

"Why orange?"

"It's the color of some of the trees in the fall. Daddy liked them and that was one of the times he went to the mountain," Timmy said.

"Let's make it orange, then we'll paint over that with the bright yellow of the other aspens, then we'll rub off some of the yellow and we'll have both. I think that would look

nice on the stones of the fireplace. What do you say?" she asked.

"Great, let's go get the frame now," he said.

"We can do that and we might even get the first coat of paint on tonight before you go to bed. How about that?" she asked. "We'll go to the craft store. We can get the paint, the brushes and the frame all at the same place."

"I want to see it after we finish the orange, then I want to help put on the yellow. I'll help you rub it off too," he said.

"Good idea. It should be dry by morning, then the next night we'll put on the yellow," she added. "We have Awanas on Wednesday, so we need to stop on it after Tuesday evening. If we don't like it, we can always paint over it and start anew on Thursday evening," she said.

That night at bedtime, Timmy asked for another Daddy story.

"Did Daddy tell you about canoeing with his father?" she asked.

"Yes, he said they had lots of fun. Pawpaw taught him how to get the canoe up, if it turned over. They played and practiced turning it over on purpose so they could turn it back up," he said.

"Did Daddy tell you about when he learned to swim?" she asked.

"Yes, he said he had been practicing in the pool but wouldn't let go of the side. One day he bounced out too deep in the lake and decided he'd better try or he was going to sink. He got a mouth full of water and started paddling. Pawpaw was standing there, so when Daddy paddled, he went right to his daddy and got tossed up into the air. Then they clapped and jumped up and down. After that, he swam all the time, he even jumped off an old log hanging out over the lake, but only after Pawpaw checked to see if the water was deep enough. Pawpaw told Daddy never to dive until he checked the bottom of the lake to be sure there wasn't a rock or branch that might hurt him. I'm going to do that too."

"I'll take you out in the lake this summer when the water gets warm enough. How would you like to go to the YMCA and practice our swimming this winter? I think that would be a nice exercise for us to try together. We might miss a few lessons because of ice or snow, but that's okay, we'll be doing it for fun and exercise," Lydia said.

"Can we? My friend Matthew goes to the Y all the time. His mom works there sometimes, so he has a free pass anytime he wants to go. Maybe we'd see him while we are there."

"You could invite him to come with us sometime or I'll call his mom and find out when they will be there. We can go at the same time. How about that?" she said.

"Could we have pizza after we swim?" Timmy asked.

"That would be great, then I wouldn't have to cook that evening." She smoothed the hair back from his forehead. Her breath caught. "You know I really love you. Sometimes you look so much like your Daddy. I wish he could see what a fine young man you're growing into. He'd be so proud, just as I am," Lydia said.

"He would be proud of me?" Timmy asked.

"You bet he would. He was very proud of you. I can remember the day we found out we were going to have a baby. He about popped his buttons. We wanted a baby so much. Then when you were born, he was really proud. He ran all over telling everyone he had a boy. He'd say, 'I have a son and he's a beaut.' Later, he'd say, 'My boy this, my boy that,' until I imagine some people got tired of hearing about "my boy," but Daddy never got tired of telling people about the things you could do," Lydia said.

"The first people he told were his parents. He called them up and said, "Guess what? I'm making you grandparents and it won't be too long. How about coming to see us about

January 10, 2000," she said.

"Did they come?" he asked.

"They sure did. They didn't come for Christmas, but they flew home to see you when you were four days old. They held you and took a million pictures. Poor little guy, you blinked all the time, because everyone took so many flash pictures. You got so you'd close your eyes when you saw the camera coming," she explained.

"Is that why you have so many pictures with my eyes squinted up?" Timmy asked.

"I think so. Finally we got you outside and then you got over squinting when the camera came around."

"Now I go on playing and let you snap away. You are going to do it anyway, so I might as well not fuss about it," he said. He sounded so much like his father. She turned her head so he wouldn't see her eyes well. She cleared her throat and took several steps away to get control.

"Are you okay, Mom?"

"Yes, son, I'm fine. I was just thinking of your daddy and all the wonderful things he's missed since he went to heaven."

"But Mom, you know things are better there than even with us," Tim said.

"Yes, even if we miss him very much, we can't ask God to bring him back from such a peaceful and wonderful place. He wanted to stay with us, but his body felt too bad, so God came to give him a perfect new body that he can enjoy."

"Do you think he sees his mountains and trees up there?" the boy asked.

"I don't know Son, but I'm sure he sees and does whatever it takes to make him happy. He'll never be sick again and he is never sad. I don't know how that works but the Bible says all will be good there."

"I'm glad," he whispered.

"Me too," Mom sighed.

The two stood with their arms around each other as they watched the beautiful sunset. Her hand rested on his curls and his head leaned into her waist.

"Let's go in, it's getting cold and we don't need to have a chill that will keep us awake tonight," Lydia said.

She turned her son toward the back door.

Timmy went straight to the video cabinet and withdrew some of his father's videos.

Lydia cringed, but sat down with him to watch some of their family times together.

At Christmas, they went by the grandparents' homes, then back to the cabin for their holiday time on Scott's Mountain. They took Tim's basketball goal and put it in the shed behind the cabin. Lydia opened only the main bedroom, master bath and kitchen.

Lydia and Archie dragged down Timmy's bed and mattress. They set it up in her bedroom. The room was large enough, the extra bed caused no problems. It made a change for Timmy and kept him close, in case he had nightmares from reminders at being back in their home, without his father. It also changed the looks of the bedroom. Lydia was less reminded of past events that had occurred there.

For their Christmas, she had purchased new matching forest inspired bedding for both their beds. The sheets were warm flannel.

She and Timmy made a game of making up the beds.

They had dry firewood stacked in their lean-to beside the cabin. She and Timmy burned the big two-story fireplace and huddled in their blankets to enjoy the peace of their home.

They hung their orange and yellow framed picture

over the fireplace. Tim held the ladder while Lydia hammered in a mortar nail between the mountain stones.

They drank hot chocolate that evening while they enjoyed the new family painting.

Lydia stayed up very late that evening thinking of her life before Scott's death.

Dear God, we're lonely. Can you fill up our hearts and lives so we don't miss Scott so much? Thank You for Your blessings. It doesn't hurt as much now, but we do miss him, we always will. I still love him and I don't want Timmy to forget his Daddy. In Your Son's name, Amen.

She sat and watched the fire until her eyes drooped. She covered herself and lay on the rug with her head propped on her arm. She slept before the fire. She still had problems sleeping in her and Scot's bed in their bedroom, even with her son now asleep there.

On Scott's Mountain, they regained peace. The forest animals had hibernated, or gone to lower elevations for the winter. Only some birds stirred. Timmy put out popcorn kernels for them and persuaded some to come to the deck railing for his hand-outs.

Their last day, Lydia and Timmy rose early to pack and prepare the cabin. Lydia did up all the laundry. They made up the beds and hung the towels back in the bathroom. Lydia cleaned the tub and sinks and put away the clean dishes.

Archie came to help them winterize the cabin again.

"You'll probably have to do all this again when you get here for summer," he said.

"Yes, but I'll know it is ready if we catch a holiday or come over a long weekend, and it makes me feel better. Guess it's some of that nesting instinct women seem to have. This is still home and I like to have it nice, even if we're not here," she said.

Lydia packed all the family videos and photo albums

into their car. She intended to have additional copies made to keep at Gunnison. She'd bring back copies for here and some of the copies would go into the bank vault for safe keeping with Scott's video messages.

Springtime?

At the beginning of April, Archie called to tell them there are not yet any signs of spring.

"A man has called and requested permission to rent the cabin. He is a minister who wishes to take a sabbatical for thirty-days. He is in need of a time for solitude and renewal after a trying time. I checked him out with the sheriff. We found no problem in the police data base."

Lydia replied, "If you think the man is responsible, allow him to have his time in our cabin." She snickered, "See Archie, God was telling me I needed to get the cabin ready, and He's always right."

"Sure He was! I'll lock up your personal items in the upstairs bedrooms and cut off the water to Tim's bathroom. I'll take Vera along. I'll let her check to see if anything personal needs to be stashed," Archie said. "She'll be better at that than I will. Is there anything special you don't wish to leave out?" he asked.

"Use your own judgement and Vera should know about the personal items. If you have time, take our clothes to the upstairs bedrooms and empty the dresser drawers. I'm sure with a resort, you are aware of what needs to be secured," Lydia said. "Have Vera check the chest of drawers too. All the dishes and appliances on the main floor are fine for the visitor to use. We emptied the refrigerator and propped the door open. You might turn it on a day or so before he comes, so the ice can freeze. Tell him he's welcome to use the washer and dryer while he's there."

Archie cleared his throat, "Uh, how are you all doing?"

"Pretty well. I think we're over the hump. We are taking swimming lessons at the Y so we can swim in the lake this summer. It's good exercise for us and something Timmy likes for us to do together." She continued, "We go to Awanas each Wednesday. Other than that, we stay home and work on school work or I paint some at night. I think we're doing better."

She continued, "Did you see the family picture over the fireplace? It was Timmy's idea to paint the frame orange and mine to add yellow and rub it off. It's supposed to look like the aspens in the fall. What do you think, does it, or is that imaginary for Timmy and me?"

"Yeah, I noticed it, but I didn't think about the aspens. I just thought it had a nice fall color, so I guess you were both right, orange and gold aspens do spell fall," Archie chuckled.

"Did you show it to Vera?" Lydia asked.

"No, but I'll point it out to her and ask her what she thinks of the painting and the frame when we go up to prepare for your visitor. I'll let her call you and give her own comments," Archie said. "I bet she'll like it. I thought you did a very fine job of capturing your family."

Archie chuckled, "God bless you both. I'd better get a move on, or Vera will think I got lost. Take care and we'll see you before long. Tell that little man hello for me. Give him a hug, if he'll still let you."

"We'll be seeing you. We think of you and Vera often," Lydia replied. "God bless, and bye for now."

A month later, Archie wrote:
The visitor came and enjoyed a quiet time. He snow shoed, walked, and sat on the deck. He went out early

most days and sometimes didn't come back until dusk. Other days, he sat on your deck and read all day. He seemed to stop only to gaze at the mountainside or look at the animals as they came by. He told me he needed this time alone with God to determine his future. When he came he didn't know whether he was going to leave the ministry, go to another place, or back to his present situation. When he left, I felt he was much healthier than when he came. That sad, forlorn look was gone from his face. I don't know what he was running from, but he looked haunted when I first met him. I think the mountain and God's creatures were very good for him. He looked rested and free when he went back to his home. I think he'll be fine now.

We look forward to your arrival in the mountains when school is out in a few months. Hope you are well and enjoy the city.

I've enclosed the balance of the man's rent money. I replaced some shingles which were blown off with our winter winds, so took out $20.00 from the check. Hope you don't mind.

By the time the minister left, it was beginning to thaw a little on your mountain's lower levels. I turned on your stand-by heat. I've been checking the cabin daily. Do you plan to come when school is out? Otherwise, I will winterize it again and close it back up. Your home awaits and if you direct, I will get it ready for you about a week before you plan to come.

Love, Archie and Vera

Summer Plans

Lydia called Archie as they began to plan for their

school vacation. Timmy was too excited to let Mom do all the talking, and listening. Both got on the phone.

"Leave the auxiliary heat on. We intend to be there the first week in June, just as soon as we can close up the house here in the city. We can't wait. Timmy asks me everyday if it is time to go yet," she said.

"Did the man go back to his church?" Timmy asked.

"Yes, he said he could handle it again. He left you a gift on the kitchen table. You'll see it when you get back. The minister wanted me to thank you for saving his faith and his life."

"Wow, that sounds like more than any human would be able to do. I hope he isn't giving us too much credit, that belongs to God," she replied.

"No, he is a man of God and knows of what he speaks," Archie answered.

"Thank you, we'll be seeing you soon. Give Vera our love. You'll hardly know Timmy, he's nearly to my shoulder now. He has taken a real growing spurt lately. I can't wait to get him out into that mountain air and get in some hiking. He keeps asking about the big bull elk. Do you ever see him?" Lydia asked.

Archie replied, "No, I haven't seen him this winter, but I do see some tracks on the trails of the mountain. Some of them are large and some are from last years' calves. I can't say for sure if they belong to the big bull. Timmy, you'll soon be able to look for yourself."

Archie could hardly contain himself. "I did find something wonderful. It's a massive antler shed on the mountain. I washed it for you. Then I set it inside your basement. I didn't want any porcupines or rodents to gnaw on it. If you want me to help, we can rig some kind of hanger when you get home."

"Did you find the other antler?" Timmy asked.

"No telling where he shed the other and it would be gone by now. The forest critters recycle antlers about as soon as they hit the ground. The antlers have minerals the other animals crave, so they go right after them. I would have liked to have found the other. I looked and looked, but could find no sign of it," Archie replied. "I've seen some fancy carvings made from antlers. We'll see when you get here. You may want to do something else with it."

Home Again

When Mom and Timmy arrived in June, they found a note on the table. There was a fresh new vase setting in the middle of the kitchen table and a green plant twined around a golden globe.

Mom read the note aloud to Timmy.

Thank you for the place. It meant the world to me. When I came, I was about to give up. It wasn't a state I wanted to continue, but I couldn't seem to bring myself out of it.

Several evening while I sat on your deck, a stately bull elk came and visited the yard. He'd stand and gaze at me for long times. He seemed to be telling me something, but I couldn't read the message.

Have you seen him before?

Mr. Archie said he hadn't, but your son had said something Archie recalled and he told me I should ask you, so I'm writing to you for information.

I've had a puzzling feeling of quiet since I stayed at your cabin.

I got my answers and I went back to my church. Things have gone exceptionally well. I still miss my family but I know they are in heaven.

I found peace on your mountain. I know it came from God.

Thank you and your son for allowing me to stay in the cabin for the month, and thanks to God for the peace I found in His creation.

You need not tell me the story of the elk, if it's too personal. I will understand but am also fascinated.

My world has awakened again for me and God's work is going well. Blessings on you and your son. Perhaps we'll meet one day.

I'd like to come again to your cabin, but don't wish to disturb you. If there is a convenient time, please let me know. I certainly appreciate your generosity.

Sincerely, Jeff Boyd

Hunting Season

When Lydia and Tim arrived at their cabin for the last days of hunting season, the first thing they saw on the kitchen table was a lush pine-scented candle. It was huge and had *bas relief* forest animals marching around the base. Behind the animals stood their majestic fur and pine trees, with blazing aspens pillowed in the draws.

"It looks like our mountain. Where did this come from?" Lydia picked up the ivory colored envelope stuck under the slate-colored candle plate.

"Open it Mom, I bet they left the note to tell us who put the candle here," Timmy said. "Probably the preacher, or Vera.."

"It could be from Vera. She or Archie are the only ones who have been here since the preacher."

Lydia read the note.

Dear Mrs. Thayer & Tim,

I saw this lovely candle in a shop window in Estes Park, Colorado, when I was at a conference. I thought immediately of your cabin in the mountains. I had to get it for you. I hope you can accept and enjoy it as much as I enjoyed your cabin.

That month I spent there opened my soul again. When the drunk driver hit my wife's car and I lost her and my daughter, I was angry with God and everyone else. I'm not sure I would have returned to my pastorate if I hadn't gone to your mountains and sat quietly to watch God's creation as it came and went from your lawn each day.

At first, I couldn't talk of my loss, but I've learned others can't help me, if they don't know the problem. All my sadness has opened doors to further ministry, so I can utilize the verse about "all things working together for the good of those who love the Lord." It isn't easy, but now seems bearable.

Thank you again for those times and the loan of your very private place. I hope that you will again share your home with me at some time when I won't interfere with your time there. I don't want to intrude, but it is a blessed place and one of the most beautiful I've ever seen. I appreciate the handiwork of your husband in the fine building *and the wonderfully creative way you have incorporated nature into the cabin and your landscaping.*

I sent this to Vera to deliver to your cabin so you'd have it this fall.

Thank you again,
Jeff Boyd

Lydia lay the letter back on the table next to the candle. She turned to put perishables into their refrigerator.

"What is landscaping, Mom?" Timmy asked.

"Well, mostly we left what trees and rocks were already here in our yard. Oh, maybe we thinned a little bit and trimmed some other spots, but mostly we used what God put there for us. Daddy did put that rough-barked arch over our fence for our rose bushes. It's all natural to our area and blends in well."

"We moved a lot of rocks, Mom, don't you remember?" Timmy asked. "We built that fence the squirrels like to sit on. It's a good place to put out nuts for them."

"Yes, we did move rocks, how could I have forgotten that? My back has never recovered," she said.

Old Friends

Archie came to see them a few hours after they drove by the resort.

"Archie, what did you think of the man who stayed in our cabin? He wrote he'd like to come again, but I wanted your input before I gave him an answer," she said.

"He didn't talk much to me and I didn't bother him. He seemed to have a lot on his mind and liked his solitude. He did his own thing and we didn't see much of him."

"As far as I could see, he took good care of the building. He cut more wood to replace what he used, he laundered the sheets and towels and put those back on when he finished. He left me a note on the bed telling me about the sheets. I could see where he chopped the wood from those downed trees at the side of your property," Archie continued.

"He seemed like a good person. I wouldn't be afraid to let him use the cabin again, if I were you," Archie said.

"He left us a note on the table that first time saying he

had found himself again and was going back to his church," Lydia said.

"He relished the mountains and their solitude. It seemed to be the medicine he needed. He wants to rent the cabin again. What do you think?" Lydia asked.

"I'm sure the money won't hurt. If it were mine, I'd say he'll take care of it again and since you won't be here yet that wouldn't be a problem. I'll be here to keep an eye on things for you, so I can't see it would hurt," Archie said.

"We found the candle you or Vera must have put on the table with his second note. He seemed much more open in his last message. Scott's Mountain seems to have been good for him. Perhaps Timmy and I will allow our home to become a ministry retreat for at least one worn-out minister."

New Family Member

Lydia drove their car to school today. She needed to go to both schools and the cold spring rain poured down.

On their way home in the deluge, Timmy cried out, "Mommy, look at the dog. He's wet and he's limping! Can we stop and help him?"

"Sure, I'll pull into this driveway. He's got on a collar, I'll see if he'll let me look at his tags," Lydia said

She turned into the driveway to a brick home and turned to caution her son. "You stay buckled in your seat and don't get out, no matter what. You hear me?" she directed

"Can't I help look at his tags?" Timmy asked.

"No, son. You know when you hurt, sometimes you don't act as nice as you usually do. Sometimes animals hurt so badly, they don't know you're trying to help them. You stay right here and let me see what I can do," Lydia said.

She put the hood of her jacket over her head and

stepped into the beating rain. She walked quietly toward the dog.

"Here boy. Come here. Let me have a look at you," she called.

The miserably wet animal turned its head and looked at her. Then it ducked its head to prevent the rain hitting its face.

She spoke softly and lowered her body to be even with the animal's line of vision. "Let me see if I can help you. I won't hurt you," she held out her hand.

The animal looked at her again and its tail made a tiny shift.

"Even though you hurt, you're trying. Let me touch you." She offered the back of her hand and took a slow step toward the animal.

The dog looked over its shoulder down the sidewalk and then shifted to look at her again.

"It's okay. I won't hurt you. Let me just come a little closer," she coaxed.

The dog shifted and seemed to make a decision. It lowered its head and took a step toward her.

"Come on boy, come on. We can do this. You don't like being wet and I can get you out of this cold rain. See, you're shivering. Are you in shock from that injured leg? Let's get in the car and get dry," she said.

The dog looked toward the car and at her again.

"Do you know what the word *car* means? Come on, I'll open the front door for you."

She patted the dog under the chin, and then turned to open the door.

She slipped a finger under the collar and read the name on the tag.

"It's a veterinarian's name. His office is very close. We'll take him there and see if the vet can fix his dog. I'm sure he's missing the dog by now," she said.

"Hurry, Mommy, the rain is blowing in and he looks cold. See him shiver," Timmy said.

"Up. Can you get up?" she coaxed the dog.

The dog made an effort but the leg was too weak. It couldn't get leverage on the slick seat even though it tried several times.

"You'll have to let me lift you. Will you do that?" she asked the dog.

"Get in doggie, get in. We're going to help you get back to your daddy. Come on doggie," Timmy called.

The dog looked at Timmy and made a lunge. Lydia boosted him from the rear, tucked in the bedraggled tail and shut the door carefully. She went around the front of her car and opened her door to find the dog already on its side on the passenger seat.

"I think he's taken car rides before. Look, Mom, how he's already laying down," Timmy said.

"Yes, he's very settled. Now let me wipe my face so I can see and get these wipers going so we can find our way to the vet's office." Lydia fumbled in the console for a tissue. She retrieved a handful and wiped the dog's face. A pink tongue flicked out to her hand.

"Good dog, you know we're trying to help you. You're being so patient. We'll soon be there," she said.

She reached for more tissues and wiped her own face.

"I'll turn on the heater and warm us all up. He seems cold and this will help until we can get him to his master and inside a building. Ready? Your seat belt still on? Okay, here we go," Lydia said.

Several turns led them to a strip mall near the school. Lydia drove as close to the door of the vet clinic as she could.

"Stay!" The dog lay its head back down on the console as she exited her door.

She opened the rear door and helped Tim run into the veterinarian's office.

"Here, I'll put you inside. Wait right here and I'll be in with our patient," she directed.

She opened the passenger door and patted the dog's hip.

"Come."

The animal laboriously rose on its good front leg and turned in the seat.

"Let me help you step down. You don't want to hurt your leg more." Lydia reached for the dog. "I'm helping, please don't bite me," she cautioned.

Patiently the dog allowed her to lift its front quarters down to the pavement. She linked her fingers in the collar and opened the door to the office.

"He came, the dog came! I knew he would. He's a good dog, isn't he Mommy?" Timmy asked.

"He sure is. Now let's see if there is someone here to help us," she said.

The dog lay back down on its belly, and held the injured paw off the floor.

Mom sighted a bell sitting on the desk. She tapped it with her finger.

A voice called out, "Sorry, I just stepped in the back to feed some of the animals. I'll be right with you."

A young man in a scrub jacket and jeans stepped from the hallway and moved behind the desk.

"What can I do for you?" he asked.

"We found this dog in the street when we were driving home. I looked at its tag and saw this address and the name Dr. Zach as owner. Can you help us? The dog has a broken leg. I can see the bone. It must be very painful, the dog keeps laying down every chance it gets," she commented.

The young man peered over the counter.

"Dixie, how did you get out? You were here a half hour ago when I let my receptionist go home early!"

The young man rushed around the corner and knelt to embrace his dog.

"Oh, my, what happened to you? I've got to get you in the OR to get that leg fixed. Now I need my assistant back to help me," he lamented.

Mom looked at Timmy, "I've been around animals all my life. I helped my husband with some injured wildlife. I think I can help, if you'll let me. Uh, that is, if my son can sit in a chair out of the way, and watch. I don't want to leave him out here by himself."

"Come on. I'll get you a surgical robe and we'll fix your boy up in a lab coat. Dixie, Come. Let's get you dried off and fixed up," the vet said.

Lydia hung her coat over the back of a chair and Timmy's on a hook by the door. She brushed the boy's forelock back off his forehead and looked him in the eye.

"Timmy, you'll have to sit very still and be very quiet. It will look like the doctor is hurting the dog, but he'll give the dog a shot and it will make it sleep while he works. The dog won't feel a thing other than a little prick when it gets the shot. You know how shots feel. Can you be very quiet so we can help this poor animal?" she asked.

"Yes, Mommy. I don't like to see it hurt. I know the doctor can fix a leg, but. . ."

"But what?" she asked.

Tears pooled in Timmy's eyes. "They couldn't fix Daddy."

Lydia spoke softly, "I know. Some things are more than people can fix. It was better for Daddy to go be with God. He was very sick and God took him home so Daddy could rest. I think the doctor can fix Dixie, she's not that sick, but we have to be quiet and let the doctor work so she'll feel better. You could say a little prayer for Dixie and her friend the doctor."

The doctor sat a chair inside the door to his operating room. He draped a green cloth over the chair and turned with a lab coat for the boy.

"Here, young man, put your arms in here and this chair is all fixed for you."

Then the veterinarian turned to her, "Mom, here's your robe. Put this cap over your hair and the mask over your nose and mouth," he said.

Lydia hurried to get the gear on.

He lifted Dixie onto the table and turned to prepare the medication.

"Pet and soothe her while I give her the anesthetic. She shouldn't have a reaction but we don't want her to struggle or fall off the table as she becomes drowsy."

The veterinarian shaved a small area of Dixie's good front leg and then swabbed the site with antiseptic. He slipped a catheter into the vein and allowed a drop of blood to appear in the clear cylinder. "Good, now for the anesthetic. I weighed her this week, so I know exactly how much she weighs and how much to give her."

Dixie panted and got an anxious look about her eyes.

Lydia patted the dog on the shoulder. She reached up to hold her hand under Dixie's head. "Easy girl, that's a good girl. Relax and let your boss do his work."

The doctor spoke to his dog, "That's a girl, just relax and let the medicine take over. This will soothe your pain and you'll feel much better when you wake up."

The dog's body slowly relaxed and her eyes closed. Her breathing deepened and she started a light snore.

Lydia removed her hand from under Dixie's muzzle and gently laid the dog's head on the table. She stretched out the dog's neck to open a good airway.

"She's out. See Timmy, she's not hurting now, so we can work on her leg without hurting her. When she wakes up, she won't remember a thing about us putting the bone back together and stitching up her skin." Lydia continued, "She's such a good dog. I've never seen one more patient when it was hurting. She trusted me enough to lay her muzzle right in my hand. She didn't fuss at all when you put the IV in."

"She is a good dog. It's too bad I have to find another home for her," the vet said.

"Why does she need another home?" Lydia asked.

"I got married about six months ago and my wife is severely allergic to her. I can't take Dixie home. I change clothes before I go home from work. Dixie has to spend her nights here at the clinic the last six months. It isn't fair to her. We've been buddies all her life and she doesn't understand why she can't be with me now. She needs a family to love her all the time," his voice sounded sad to Lydia.

Timmy started to stand up, "Mommy, can we have her?"

"Timmy, don't forget to sit. We mustn't stir up any germs or dust to get into Dixie's wounds," Lydia said.

"Sorry, I forgot. Can we Mommy? Can we?"

"This is too sudden. Let me think about it, Timmy," Mom whispered.

The young vet turned to her, "My assistant has rubber gloves here in this box. See if you can pull a pair on without touching the outside. You won't have to come in contact with Dixie's wound, so you don't have to be totally sterile but I may need you to hold something for me and it's best we stay as germ-free as we can."

Lydia pulled on a pair of the lavender gloves.

"Mom, those are pretty. They match your sweater," Timmy said.

The vet turned with his instruments. "Okay, let's

begin. The first thing I'll do is clean the wound and be sure we've got all the debris and fur out. I'm going to use this dental pick to spray out the site with an antiseptic solution. Hold that basin under her wound. I hope I don't spray you, but please forgive me if I do. Do you want a pair of goggles, just in case?" he asked.

"I'm fine." Lydia maneuvered the basin under the leg where it hung from the table.

"Here goes," he said.

Bits and pieces of leaves and dirt fell into the basin with the soapy solution. After several minutes, he raised the limb and examined the underside.

"It looks as good as it can. Let me change this solution and rinse a bit, then we'll be ready to start aligning the bones. It looks like a clean break, so we should be able to adjust things without any pins. To be certain, I'll take an x-ray with my portable machine."

He turned to empty the pan into the stainless steel sink, then picked up a clean basin and handed it to Lydia.

"Do the same as we did before. That's it. Good job," he commented through his mask.

He took the second basin away and used sterile gauze to blot out the excess water.

The doctor arranged his x-ray plate and wheeled over the machine.

"You and Timmy step outside the door until I get this picture taken. I'll signal when you can return."

Tim looked through the window in the door and saw the veterinarian put on a black apron. The man stepped to the other side of his dog.

Lydia pulled the boy in front of her own body and turned her back to the door. "Timmy, turn your head and look the other direction for a minute. We don't want to get any scattered rays in our face," Lydia directed.

They heard a zap, when the veterinarian punched a remote button.

They heard a muffled call, "Now you can come back in. I'm all set. I'll take these into the dark room and have a look."

In a few minutes he returned. "It looks good. I don't see any bone chips or solids in the wound. The break is on a diagonal and it looks like it would fit back together in good shape."

Timmy placed himself in his chair again. He gathered the lab coat around his legs and tucked it under.

The vet directed, "Mom, you go to her back and hold around her chest while I maneuver the bones into position." A hand on each side of the break, the doctor grunted as he pulled the bones.

"Got it! That went back together well, so she should heal well"

"If we don't have any infection set in, she'll be fine. I'll stitch up the wound and then we'll put her in a temporary cast. I can't entirely bandage the surface area over her wound, she may need further work if I didn't get out some foreign matter. I didn't see any stray bone chips, I'm predicting the bone will heal quickly. She probably won't even have a limp."

He worked quickly as he talked.

"You'd make a good instructor Dr. Zach. You've been teaching Timmy and I ever since you started this procedure," Lydia said.

"I'd like to teach at some time down the road, but now, I'm getting my practice going and with a new family, I need to be home more," he said. "We're expecting a baby in about six months and I want to be a hands-on father. Is your husband good with Timmy?"

"He was, very good." Lydia didn't want the young

man to be embarrassed. "He died from cancer the spring Timmy was five. I went back to teaching after about two years. We had to move from our mountain cabin to the city for a part of the year, but I think we've adjusted fairly well."

"I'm sorry, one doesn't expect the death of younger people and I assumed facts I shouldn't have. There are many single mothers who come into my practice to have their critters cared for. It isn't safe to assume anything," he said.

"That's all right. It is only natural to make assumptions," she soothed.

They worked in silence for a few moments.

"It will take a few minutes for her bandages to soak in the plaster solution. That will give us time to see if there's any more swelling or bleeding." He lifted Dixie to feel all over her body for any other problems and found none. He looked at his watch and noted the time on a marker board. He gave the cast bandages a stir and turned back. He crossed his arms over his chest and stood with his back against the counter.

"How long is it going to take for her to be healed?" Lydia asked.

"I'd say the cast should come off in six to eight weeks, then she won't be able to run and be too active for another month. After that, she can do whatever she wants. Why do you ask?" he said.

"Can I talk to you privately?" Lydia asked.

"Sure, after I get the cast on, I'll lay her in a recovery cage so she can wake up quietly. I don't want her to struggle and fall off this table, or leap down on that leg. I think the casting bandages are ready, I'll begin," he said.

Lydia held the basin with the casting materials while the doctor wound the gauze around Dixie's leg. He left the area over the stitches covered only with a gauze pad and wrapped above and below the two joints.

"There, I think that's got her in good shape. I'll put her

in a recovery cage and then get back to her as soon as I clean up this mess and get my OR ready for the next patient. We never know when we'll have an emergency, so we need to be prepared with a clean room. I have another OR that is ready, but I prefer this one. I keep more equipment in here. I can't leave it until later, because emergencies don't occur by appointment, just like this one with Dixie."

"Timmy, can you go into the hall and play with that kitty we saw out there? I'll help the doctor clean up this mess, then we'll go have our dinner," Lydia said.

The little boy stepped out the door and hiked up the long lab coat.

The doctor hurried to the boy's side. "Here, son, we can take that off now. You won't need this to play with my kitty. You were very good in there. Thank you for helping us out so well," the vet said.

"I'm glad Dixie is going to be okay. My Daddy was very sick and he didn't get well," Timmy said.

"I'm sorry, but sometimes I can't help the animals that come in. I try, but they're just too sick," the vet said.

"That's what Mommy said. Daddy went to be with Jesus, so he wouldn't hurt anymore."

"That's right. Now you go play with Charmin and we'll get this place ship shape again." The doctor closed the door behind the little boy and looked through the window to see the little boy squat and start to pet his cat. He could see the little boy was quiet and allowed the cat to come to him. He didn't rush or try to pick her up. Tim wiggled his fingers on the floor and the lazy old cat softly patted the finger as it came near.

Lydia moved toward the door.

"They're fine. He knows how to be quiet around the animals and he's got ole Charmin chasing his finger. She won't hurt him, she doesn't have claws. Someone brought her in that way. She and Dixie are our resident greeters for the office. She's friendly to about everyone."

He turned to pick up the soiled drapes and other equipment.

"Now, what was it you wanted to discuss?" he asked.

"We have a home in the mountains my husband built for us. He was a forest ranger and into research, but he's gone now, so we come to the city during the winter for school, so we can get out of the mountains when the snows come. We go to the mountains every summer and most holidays."

She continued, "We have fifteen steps up to the house we live in here during the winter. We might be able to take your dog, if you can take care of her for a few weeks until she's able to get around a bit better. By summer she'd be able to get up to our deck in the mountains. We are not wealthy and I assume this bill to repair her leg will be rather expensive?" Lydia asked.

" There will be no bill for this broken leg or for her. I can see you are kind people and Dixie seems to have accepted you both. If you'll take her, I'd be very happy. This was an accident and I have no idea how she got out, or why. Normally, she isn't one to roam around. She must have gone out with my assistant for some reason. But surely Janet didn't notice Dixie or she would have brought her back inside. Maybe she followed Janet."

He continued, "Dixie is fully house-trained and a good dog. She isn't boisterous or wild in the house, so she won't damage your belongings. As you can see, she is very good with kids. She tends to want to mother them and most small critters that come into the clinic. That's been helpful when we've had some young puppies or kittens. She takes right over, if we'll let her."

Lydia looked thoughtful, "School won't be out until the end of May. We can pick her up sooner than that, if you think she's ready. Can she stay alone while we're at school?"

"Sure, she's accustomed to the whole night alone. You'll just reverse that time." He continued, "I'd appreciate you getting her in a few weeks. It would probably be good if she has time to adjust to you before you go to the mountains. That would give her time to bond and be in an established family. I wouldn't want her to try to come home to me after you got farther away from here," he said.

"We would keep her on leash here in the city. We do have a small area fenced in the back yard here," Lydia said.

"She is a jumper, so your fence would need to be at least six feet tall," he said. "She shouldn't be landing on that leg for a time either."

Lydia looked anxious, "I'm sure our fence is no more than five feet, but if we were with her, would she attempt to escape?"

"I think she'd be fine as long as you're there too, but if left alone, she might try it," he said.

"I see no reason she'd need to be alone in the yard. We'd take her out on a leash until she bonds with us. Then while she plays with Timmy, she could be loose," she said.

"You'd need to play it out as it goes," he said. "Use the leash while in the fenced area at first. When she's engaged and you see she's satisfied, take her off leash for a time. If she is calm and connected, leave her for longer periods of time. Gradually lengthen distance and time until she obeys you and your son. Teach Tim at the same time. He will need to learn to give commands seriously. Dixie will learn she can trust him and know he is her master. Never forget she is good at the "stay" command, even at a distance. Should she get out, speak the word and she'll halt. That could save her life if she's loose. Impress that upon your son from the very start."

"In the mountains, we'll have to see how she adapts to other animals. We have many that come into our yard. We feed the birds and some of the other little critters. We also have a huge bull elk that comes at least once a year. We like to sit on the deck and watch him as he comes down the mountains. If she barks, we could leave her in the house while he's around, but that's not a frequent occurrence," Lydia explained.

"She'll be quiet, if you tell her to. You can tell her to down, stay, quiet, or hush to achieve that," the vet said. "The animals will be no problem. Sounds like she'd have a wonderful life and a lot more fun with you folks than she has in my life now, locked up in the clinic by herself," he said.

The two had completed their clean up.

"I need to spray down the table and turn on the air exchange. Can you step out of the OR?"

He sprayed down the table and floors, flicked a switch and stepped out of the fumes.

As Lydia came from the operating room, Timmy said, "Look Mommy, look at Charmin. She likes me. I found her feather and she followed it around. She can even jump into the air almost as tall as I am. She tries to catch it." He demonstrated the cat's antics with a beautiful peacock feather.

"Are you ready to go home?" Mom asked.

"Uh, are we going to get Dixie?" the little boy asked.

"We need to talk about that. How about we go for pizza and see what we decide?" Lydia said.

"I already know, I want her," Timmy said.

"I'd like to have her too, but there are responsibilities that go with owning a dog. We need to discuss all those and think very seriously if we'd be able to do all the things we need to make her happy," Mom said. "Our house here isn't very large and she'd need some room to exercise. She'll need a place to sleep and live during the day while we're gone to school."

"Mom, does she know about going outside for potty?"

I'd hate to clean that up in our house," Timmy asked.

"Me too, but Dr. Zach says she is a very well house trained dog. She doesn't tear up furniture or clothes, but we wouldn't leave things laying around to tempt her either. It wouldn't be good to leave our garbage lid open or our food on the table. She's going to need food good for dogs and fresh water. She shouldn't be fed off our table, that would make her a nuisance and people food isn't that good for her."

Dr. Zach entered the hallway, "Thank you for your help with Dixie and for finding her. I would have been very worried when she didn't show up at closing time.." He turned to tidy his desk. "Let me know what you decide. Timmy, you can come visit her if you want. She'll be up and about in a day or so and will welcome company by then," the vet said.

He turned to Lydia, "Could you leave me your phone number and address, so I can call if there are changes?"

"Sure, I'll write it here on this pad at your desk," Lydia said.

"We'll see you soon. I'll call you about the other," Lydia added.

When they got into the car and headed for the pizza village, Timmy made plans.

"How about toys? She'd need toys to play with while we're gone so she won't get bored," Timmy added.

"You're right, she will need all that. It is going to cost us something to feed her, get her toys, fix her a bed, get her a leash, and all the other things she will need," Lydia added.

"Maybe she already has toys and a leash. I saw some at the doctor's office. A green leash was hanging by the back door," Timmy said.

"Maybe she does have some of those things. We should ask Dr. Zach what she needs and I'm sure he'll tell us if she already has some of those things," Lydia said.

Mom pulled her car to the parking place closest to the

Pizza Village entrance. The two ran through the light rain and scurried in the door.

"Let's go wash our hands before we sit down, then we can talk while they fix our pizza," Mom directed.

Timmy eagerly walked to the door. He could hardly wait to discuss *his* new dog.

"When can we go see her again?" Timmy asked when he came from the restroom.

"I have a teachers' meeting after school tomorrow, but we probably could go the next day. The doctor said she would feel better by that time. Taking a day off will give her time to get her cast dried out and she'll be fully awake by then. She'll feel better in a day or so. I expect tomorrow, she'll just want to rest and sleep a lot. She may be a little groggy from the sleep medicine the doctor gave her. He may have to give her some pain medications too, if he thinks her leg hurts her."

"I can't wait to tell the kids in school tomorrow, and church on Sunday. Wow, we're getting our very own dog!" Tim crowed.

Two days later, they went to visit Dixie at her owner's clinic. She wasn't in the front room when they entered.

"She has a slight temperature," Dr. Zach said, "That is fairly common for an animal with a wound. I'm giving her an antibiotic, in case there is some infection, but I feel she will be herself again very soon."

Mom took Tim's hand, "We won't bother her today. She needs her rest."

Timmy grabbed her hand. When they got outside, he said, "Is Dixie going to die too?"

Lydia clutched him to her, "I don't think so. Do you want to go back and ask Dr. Zach?"

"No, Mommy, but I don't want her to die like Daddy did," Timmy said.

"How about we pray for her? Would you like to do that?" Lydia asked.

"I'm afraid," Timmy whispered.

"Why, Son?" Lydia asked.

"Daddy didn't live after we prayed for him," he said.

"Sometimes our prayers are not answered just the way we want, but they are answered. We just don't understand at the time." Lydia's thoughts ran silently through her mind. *My prayers didn't come out very well either. Oh, God, help me, help my son, when I don't know the answers.*

The next day, Lydia called the veterinary clinic for a progress report on Dixie.

"She's doing fine," the attendant said.

"We'll be in day after tomorrow to see her, if that's okay? My son wants to see her again," Lydia said.

"That'll be great, she's waiting to see you," she said.

On the fourth day, Dixie greeted Timmy at the reception room door. She had a green cast on her leg. Her foot in the cast, tapped on the floor as she walked toward him. She seemed to have no problems with her injured leg.

Timmy fell on his knees to hug her. She licked his face.

"She likes me, Mommy. See she kisses me," he said.

"I do believe she does," Mom agreed.

Dixie turned to Lydia and licked her hand.

"She likes you too," the little boy said.

The young veterinarian came from the back hallway.

"There you are. I think she's been waiting for you. If you'd like, you can snap on her leash and take her for a short walk back of this building. It would be good for her and you can start getting accustomed to caring for her. Her leash is on the nail by the door," he said.

"I knew it. I told Mommy her leash was the green one by the door. It matches her collar," Timmy said.

"This is how you snap it on. I don't know if you can open it by yourself, but Mom needs to be with you outside anyway, so that's okay. Your mother can take it off when you come inside," the vet said.

"Are you ready, Mom? Let's go. See, she's already at the door. She knows we're going outside," Timmy said.

"Don't let go of her leash, "Lydia cautioned as the threesome exited the clinic.

Three weeks later when they went to retrieve Dixie to take her to her new home with them, the young veterinarian knelt down and gave the dog a hug. He snapped on her leash.

"Be a good girl." He rose, handed the end to the boy. He looked into Timmy's face. "Please bring her back to see me in three weeks to get her cast off. Then anytime you wish. Don't forget to bring her in for her shots every March." He looked at Lydia, "If she has any medical needs, I'm prepared to cover those for you. Just come in or make an appointment anytime we're open. You have my emergency number on my card too. Here's six months' worth of her heart worm and her flea and tick medications. The instructions are written on the two boxes."

"Please give me details I need to know as to her age and any likes, dislikes, or habits we need to know about to make her the happiest dog in the world," Lydia said.

"Delighted. In fact, I've written out a whole page of instructions and her life history. She's a very well-bred dog. I spayed her because I see so many unwanted little critters, I didn't want to add to the numbers, plus we have so many animals coming in here, I didn't want her to be a problem in the clinic. In some ways, it is healthier for her to prevent problems down the way with cancers caused by hormones. Well, you may not have wanted my lecture, but that's how I feel and it's hard not to give forth every chance I get. Sorry about that," the veterinarian added.

"That's fine. I think this will make things easier for us all. If there was a litter, Timmy would want to keep them all. One dog is fine, but we don't need a whole menagerie," Lydia said.

Lydia took the papers, a brush, and a dog bowl with "Dixie" written on it.

"I can't wait, let's go Mom!" Timmy turned to Dr. Zach, "She's gonna really like her new bed, it's right by mine and she has a new water dish and . . . just all kinds of stuff. Thank you, Dr. Zach."

The vet put his hand on Tim's shoulder, "She'll like that. She was lonely at night here in the clinic. I left her loose and she took care of things, but there's nothing like her very own boy to sleep by. You take care of her and she'll take care of you, Tim."

The boy and dog started toward the door.

Timmy turned back and threw his arms around Dr. Zach's waist for a big hug. The veterinarian hugged the boy to him.

The pair turned to the door again. Dixie looked back over her shoulder at her former master, then jauntily walked out with her boy.

The young vet turned away.

"Thank you, Dr. Zach," Lydia said. "Timmy has had some real problems with nightmares since his father is gone. I think Dixie will be an answer to my prayers on how to help him with some of his feelings. I've had to sleep in the same room with him a lot, and at times, he's kind of reverted back to his babyhood. It will be better for him to become more independent. Thank you again. You don't know how much this means to us both," Lydia's voice caught.

He replied gruffly, "Yeah, I think I do. Take care, and enjoy her, she's a good one."

"I better go, they're trying to get in the car and I don't want another broken leg. God bless you," Lydia wiped a tear and gave him a quick hug.

Acquiring an Education

"Mom, look."

Lydia stopped the sweep of her leaf rake and looked at the two friends.

"We're playing freeze tag. Look at Dixie. *Freeze!*" Tim yelled.

Dixie stopped with one foot in the air and her head turned toward the boy. Her tail gave one sweep before she froze that too.

"Marvelous." Lydia looked for a minute and asked an obvious question, "How do you get her unfrozen?"

"Come. See, she's unfrozen and ready to play some more."

"How does she freeze you?" Mom asked.

"I let her touch me, then I stand still until she moves," the boy replied.

"You've got it all worked out. That looks like fun."

"Come, join us!" he said.

"Okay. *Freeze!*" Lydia said.

The pair stopped in mid-stride. Tim was off-balance. He tumbled over into her pile of leaves.

"No fair, you unfroze," she taunted.

"No, I'm still frozen, I'm not moving," Timmy said.

"Call Dixie let her come play in your leaves," she said.

"Come. You come too Mom," Timmy yelled.

The dog joined the boy in his pile of leaves. Lydia dropped a shower of red and gold on them until she couldn't see the pair.

They are too quiet, I wonder what they are doing?

"Okay guys, what's up?" she asked.

The pair burst from their haven and showered her with their burst of energy. The three threw leaves until her mound of raked leaves was totally scattered again.

"Boy, that's fun," Tim said.

"Yes, but now we need to rake them all back up again," Lydia said.

"Ahhh, Mom. Let the wind blow them away," he coaxed.

"Okay, we'll come back out tomorrow evening and you all can play again. Let's go in for a bowl of hot soup," she directed.

A few more days and the boy had Dixie's freeze perfected. He started to say, "Stay!" To make her hold the pose longer.

One day Mom said, "She looks like she's posed. I imagine the kids at school would like to draw her. Maybe I'll get permission to bring her to one of my art classes and see how it works out."

After another month of perfecting their freeze tag routine, Lydia spoke to Tim, "I've been teaching animal drawing to the fourth grade class. I'll ask my building principal if I can bring Dixie to one of the art classes. If she does well, then perhaps I'll take her to your building," Lydia told Tim during their evening meal. "I'll ask him tomorrow at our teachers' meeting. The class is before lunch and I change buildings at mid-day so I'll bring her home then. I think she'd like it. What do you think, Tim?" she asked.

"Neato, she'll like that. I wish I could be out and go with you, but Miss Smith says we need to be at school everyday we're not sick."

"She's right. School is important and we don't want to miss a thing. I'll tell you what the principal says when I get home tonight."

Lydia approached Mr. Madison after the meeting. "May I have a moment of your time?"

"Certainly. What can I do for you?" he asked.

"I've been teaching animal drawing to the fourth grade classes. I was wondering if I could bring in a live animal for their final project?" Lydia asked.

"I don't know, the liability is very expensive and it's not our policy to allow animals in the school," he stated.

"This is a golden retriever, she's very well- mannered, she plays with my little boy all the time and she's very tolerant. She is also calm and very patient. Her shots are up to date." Lydia talked fast to get in all the gold stars she could for Dixie.

"My son has taught her to play freeze tag. He says 'Freeze' and she will 'Stay' frozen until we release her. I think she would be an ideal subject for the children to draw. Could I give her a little try? I could arrange for my aide to be present and I would take the dog out, if she acts in any way nervous. You could come observe too. I think it would be good for the children."

Lydia continued, " Some schools use service dogs to calm the children. It seems to help them learn. She's not certified yet, but I think she'd pass, if she were tested." Lydia looked at Mr. Madison expectantly.

"Well, if you tell me exactly when and I have time to observe at that time, we can give it a try. Don't disappoint me, or we'll both be in trouble," he stated.

"Great, how about Thursday at ten-forty-five, the hour before that class has lunch?" she asked.

"Don't forget to give them time to wash their hands before they go to lunch," he said. "There's that e-coli scare from petting zoos. That's another thing to worry about."

"We have sinks, antiseptic soap, and paper towels in the art room, so that's no problem. We'll be sure to time it carefully. Thank you, Mr. Madison," Lydia said.

"I'll see you Thursday. I'll put it in my Blackberry® right now." He walked away with his head down, punching in the time and date for the experimental dog drawing in the art room.

Lydia was nervous on the appointed day for Dixie's classroom visit. Tim gave instructions as they drove to his school, then she and Dixie planned to walk to her art classroom at ten-fifteen, Thursday morning.

Lydia slipped Dixie's leash on. She wanted to enter the hallway when all the children were in classrooms.

Dixie sensed her nervousness and danced on the leash. "Let's have a potty break before we go in the back entrance." Lydia gathered her plastic bag and led Dixie to a suitable site.

"Good dog," Then Lydia cautioned, "Heel. Patience, Dixie, we don't want to get into trouble."

Once in the classroom, she released Dixie to check out the room. Dixie walked around, sniffed at the paint jars and glue on the shelves, checked out the seats, and then lay down next to Lydia's desk and chair.

"Good dog, you're going to like this," Lydia said.

Lydia placed each of the children's sketch pads at their regular seats and arranged drawing pencils and hand pencil sharpeners at strategic intervals.

She looked over the class room and at precisely ten-forty, Lydia snapped on Dixie's leash. The bell rang and twenty students filed in.

A collective, "Oh, a dog!" arose from the group as they entered the room.

Lydia directed, "Take your seats at the tables. I've moved all the seats so you can see our subject. Today, we are going to draw a live animal. This is Dixie. She's a Golden Retriever. My son has taught her to play freeze tag, so I'll freeze her for a few minutes. Draw quickly. It won't be fair to make her pose for too long. I will release her from the pose after about five minutes, so you can fill in detail, then she'll pose again. We'll see how quickly you can capture her likeness. If we have time left after the drawing, you'll have a chance to pet her. Be on your best behavior for her. Mr. Madison will be along soon too. Flip up your first clean page and begin as soon as she's frozen into her pose."

Lydia led Dixie to a low table. "Up, that's a girl. Pose. Freeze. Stay."

"Wow," several of the children said.

"Draw, don't waste time," Lydia directed.

She walked around, assisted children as they needed.

After a few minutes, Mr. Madison eased into the room and stood at the back.

Lydia passed him, "Do you want a chair?" she whispered.

"No, I can see better this way. So far, this is marvelous. I haven't seen them so quiet in a long while," he whispered back.

No noise could be heard in the quiet room. After five minutes, Lydia spoke. "I'm going to give Dixie a rest now. She will lay here on the platform and you can add details to her face, hair, whatever you see that you think needs to be in your drawing. After a few minutes, I'll have her pose again. Please continue to work."

Lydia stepped to the platform. She touched the dog's

shoulder. "Dixie, down. At ease."

The dog collapsed and rested her head on her paws. By the time another five minutes had passed, Dixie gave a snore.

The children tittered.

"She is relaxed," Lydia said. "Dixie, Up!" The dog arose and looked at her mistress. "Pose. Freeze."

Again the children and Mr. Madison marveled at the dog's obedience.

"Don't forget to work on your drawing. We have another fifteen minutes, then we'll wash up for lunch," Lydia said.

Dixie continued to respond to directions. When given the next ease, Lydia snapped on her leash and led her by each child for a pat on the head, or Dixie shook hands with those who offered their palm toward her leg.

"Put your sketch pad back in your cubby hole and line up at the three sinks. Don't forget to use soap so you'll be ready for lunch," Lydia directed.

She led Dixie to her desk and put her on a down, stay, while she supervised the lines.

"When you're finished washing, stand in line at the door. I'll take you to the lunch room. Jerry, you missed the trash can. Okay, ready to go?" She opened the door and led the children down the hall.

Dixie remained beside her desk in the classroom.

Mr. Madison looked after the children and walked over to Dixie. He stood looking at the dog.

Dixie raised her head and looked at his face.

"Come," he said.

Dixie stayed in position but cocked her head.

Lydia stepped back into the room. She saw Mr. Madison squatted in front of Dixie. He spoke again, "Come."

Dixie looked beyond him at Lydia. "Dixie, okay."

Lydia said.

Dixie arose and with great dignity approached Mr. Madison's outstretched hand.

"Wow, I'm like the kids. I am amazed," he said as he fondled her ear. "She is some kind of dog. You can bring her anytime you wish."

Lydia spoke, "Thank you. I knew she'd be great. She is an amazing dog. She's been a real lifeline for my son since the loss of his father. I was at my rope's end trying to figure out what would help him the most. Dixie took care of that for both of us."

Mr. Madison was in awe. "Thank you for bringing her. I think the children saw what good behavior is all about. They were good today too. She's a good influence on them."

"I've read several articles about dogs in classrooms. Some rooms have resident animals that stay with the children all day. It seems to calm the children and their grades improve. I think that's a good idea with the right dog and Dixie is wonderful in such situations," Lydia said. "One would need to check carefully to be certain none of the children have a fear of animals before the dog was introduced. In the long run, I think a quiet, patient dog could bring most children out of their fear."

"Is Dixie available for classroom use in other rooms?" he asked.

"Timmy and I would have to think about it. She is too important to our family to overwork her. I think we might allow her to come, on a limited basis, but not for all day. She needs R and R too and she's very busy in the evenings and on weekends with my son," Lydia said. "She is very active and you didn't see her exuberance. She might be a little feisty for some classrooms, unless the teacher was also trained."

Lydia returned Dixie to their home on her way to the other school.

"See you later, Dixie. You were such a good dog today. Have a good nap and we'll be home before you know it. I love you, girl," Lydia cooed as she ruffled the dog's ears and planted a kiss on atop Dixie's head.

"See you later," she shut the door and hurried to her car.

That evening driving home, Lydia spoke to Tim.

"Dixie did really well at drawing class today. I think I'll talk to your principal tomorrow and see if you can take her to your school. Would you like to take her for *Show and Tell*, if your teacher and principal agree?" she asked. "I'll ask Mr. Madison to call and give his description of Dixie."

"Oh, yeah. That would be really cool," Tim said. "What did she do today at the art class?"

"Mostly she posed and froze, or then I let her be at ease, so the kids could draw her fur and tail. She acted perfectly. The principal was impressed and wanted her to come to a classroom and stay all the time. I told him we'd think about it, but I didn't think we wanted her to have a full-time job, she already has a big job taking care of us at night and she needs some time off too," Lydia said.

"I'd like to have her in my classroom all the time, but she does need time to rest. I think the kids would pile all over her and that might wear her out," Tim said. "I don't think we should share her all the time, but I don't mind if she goes once in a while."

"I think that's about right. I'll let Mr. Madison set up a few times that suit my schedule and we'll give it a try, maybe a couple of times each month," she said.

If your principal agrees, she can do that at your school too. You might end up out of kindergarten to supervise Dixie if we don't watch. You don't want to miss your class either, so we won't do it often. Okay?" Mom asked.

"Suits me. I think Dixie would like it sometimes," he commented.

The next week, Lydia spoke to her principal, "Mr. Madison, you pick a classroom when I have a free hour and we'll try it a couple of times per month. Tim and I agreed we don't want her to burn-out with an overload on her patience. The children will be so excited at first, they won't settle down. Drawing required them to stay in their seats, but I can imagine some wanting to pet her all day and never accomplishing any school work. Probably a free reading time or something casual would be a better setting for short times."

"She has Tim's school too, so between the two, we might end up doing it about once each week. I think that would be enough. I've read about dogs being used in behaviorally challenged classrooms. I think that would be good, but I certainly wouldn't want Dixie injured or hurt. Those would need very close supervision. We aren't against her in those classrooms but I want you to know our concerns."

After preliminary training and work with the teachers, Dixie became a frequent class visitor and did go with Tim for Show and Tell on his day. He was the proudest kid in the room when he showed her abilities. The children liked the freeze tag best of all. At recess, they all played the game with her.

Special rules were set for the game time. With Lydia's approval, only the one who was "it" was allowed to freeze her. The others had to stand back to prevent utter confusion.

Lydia was concerned Dixie might not settle down when they returned to the classroom, but when all became quiet, Dixie rested on Tim's mat.

Lydia, Tim, and Dixie all slept soundly on school nights. The trips to school and the excitement were tiring for the whole family.

Lydia was beginning to sleep through the night. Tim had done so since Dixie came into their lives.

On Dixie's first night with him, he had been so excited, he kept waking up to see if she was really there, but after that, he'd reach over, almost in his sleep, pat her and fall right back to sleep. On his bad nights, she climbed into his bed, but those times had become fewer and fewer as the year advanced.

If Lydia awakened and peeped into their room, Dixie would raise her head, look at Lydia, then Tim, lay her head back and appear to say, "I've got it covered, you can rest now."

Lydia did. Her memories of Scott grew more pleasant and the horrible times of his illness faded.

Home Again

When Lydia and Tim arrived back at their mountain the following June, Dixie spent the first few minutes sniffing around the lawn. Tim was excited and she absorbed the excitement of the family.

"Look on the roof next to the chimney, Mom. It's a different color," Tim noted. " It has bright new shingles."

They noted other obvious signs of work on the cabin. A fresh coat of stain beaded with drops of moisture on the front porch and deck floors. When they walked inside, the house smelled fresh and inviting.

"It looks good, Mom. I'm so glad to be back. Somehow, this seems more like home than our house in

Gunnison," Tim said.

"I agree, there's no place like home. Let's go for a walk." Lydia held out her hand.

"Do we need to put our stuff away?" Tim asked.

"Let's wait. We've got the whole summer and no clocks to watch. Let's go see Mr. Archie and Vera."

As soon as the two walked to their friends' home, they ran to meet Archie where he stood with his arms open.

"Welcome, welcome! I'm so glad you're back. My, Tim, you are going to be bigger than your mom before we know it. Let me holler for my wife. She'll be upset if she doesn't get to see you soon," Archie said.

The four greeted.

"Archie, did you seal the deck?" Lydia asked.

"No, when I went up one day, it had just been done. Your guest took care of it," he answered.

"Did he get money for the sealer?" Lydia asked.

"No, he didn't ask and by the time I noticed it, he was already gone," Archie replied.

"I still have his address, I'll have to write and ask for the bill, but I'll check by the hardware store first. Maybe he charged it," Lydia noted.

"He might have, but I think he did it to thank you and Tim for the loan of your home," Archie said.

"How was he doing this time?" Lydia asked.

Vera replied, "He was a different person this time. He came down several times to visit with us and we had him over for dinner. He brought along some trout from the stream up the mountain and we had a fish fry another night. We even invited some of the other neighbors from our church group. He fit right in and seemed to have a good time. He came down to church a couple of times."

"I'm glad to hear that." She looked up the mountain

toward her husband's memorial.

"Our mountain seems to have a very healing quality for many of us. Tim and I had a good winter and we've gained a new family member. I guess you saw Dixie before she took off to check out your yard? We found her injured one day when we came from school and her owner fixed her up for us. He had to give her up, so Tim and I inherited her. She is a very welcome member of our family. She has solved some of the problems I mentioned earlier to Vera. She's also very well-behaved, so she won't bother the animals around our places. We're all ready to enjoy our summer. I can't wait to get out and move around."

Lydia raised her arms and took a deep breath.

"I love it. The air smells so good!" she said.

"We're glad you're back. Give me another hug," Vera reached for Tim.

" We'll head out tomorrow and we may even camp out overnight. I wanted to warn you, so you won't worry if you don't see us toward night. We want to take full advantage of our time to be free and carefree this summer."

Archie signaled out of Tim's hearing, "Take along your pistol."

"For any particular reason?" Lydia asked.

"No, but there are mommy bears up there and a few other possibilities, better to be prepared than run into more than you can handle," Archie advised.

"I don't want to shoot anything," Lydia said.

"I know, but a pistol makes some noise and if you have a problem, that may be all you need to keep things under control," Archie added.

"You're right, I'll take along Scott's pistol. I'll put it in my backpack under the clothes, so Tim won't worry about it. I haven't had it out for months, but guess I'd better clean it tonight after Tim hits the sack."

"It might be good if you went out back and fired off a few rounds to be sure your ammunition is still good," Archie commented.

"That might awaken Tim and scare him. He's been really worried about anyone shooting the animals while we were gone," she said.

"Take him out back and shoot a few tin cans off your clothesline pole. Aim into the hillside," Archie replied.

"Guess I'd better do as you say. I need to show him how to use his dad's pistol. I'll show him how to clean it after lunch. Don't worry if you hear some noises this afternoon, remember it was your suggestion," she patted Archie's shoulder.

"You better check to see if your dog is gun shy too. If she is, you might want to leave her at the cabin, rather than have her afraid and run off up in the mountains. You don't want to lose her there if she becomes frightened."

"No, I don't want to comb the whole mountain to find her. I'll introduce her to the noise gradually and tell her it's all right. She does seem to understand well when we tell her, okay," Lydia said.

"Did you see the gift on your table?" Vera asked.

"No, we rushed in, dumped our bags and came straight down here. I made a quick pass upstairs, but I didn't really look around much. A gift, you say?" Lydia said.

"Yes, the gift is lovely and suits your cabin well," Vera added.

"We'll check it out when we go back. Come see us if you have a minute." She turned, "Tim and Dixie, you all ready to go?" she asked.

The pair took off running back up the trail.

"Guess you got your answer," Archie said.

"I had better get a move on. They'll be there before I take two steps. We'll see you. Oh, I love you two. Take care." She spoke over her shoulder from the first plateau on the trail.

When they got back to the house, Timmy looked at the dining table. "It's a cabin, Mom," he said. "He left a note again."

Lydia strolled to the table, her curiosity raised.

"Why, it's a tin of maple syrup in a log cabin shape. It looks like a miniature of ours, except there's no dormers. We'll have some on our pancakes in the morning and after we empty the tin, you can use it with your toys," she commented. "I used to have these when I was a little girl."

"Neato," Tim said.

Lydia wrote their minister visitor.

Thank you for the gift. We enjoyed the syrup on our pancakes. Tim is now using the tin with his animals and trucks. He's making good use of it.

You certainly don't need to leave gifts, as you pay us well for the time you spend at our cabin.

I need your bill for all the work you did at the cabin.
                                    Sincerely, Tim and Lydia

He replied: *I have no bill, the work was enjoyable for me. I so appreciate your generosity in allowing me the use of your property. I can't thank you enough. Who can put a price on God's creation and His peace?*
                                    Thanks Again, Jeff Boyd

That fall, after the first months of school, Tim, Lydia, and Dixie returned for the last days of the hunting season on their mountain.

The third morning before dawn, the three went out on the deck and settled to wait for their messenger. Tim cautioned Dixie that she must be quiet. He practiced her freeze stance until Dixie grew bored and lay down with her head on her paws. She dozed.

Again the bull elk came down the mountain at dawn on the day after the hunting season ended.

As he advanced with the sunrise, Tim cautioned the alert Dixie, "Stay." The dog gazed toward the trees but was not anxious. She had been in the forest many times during the summer and had grown accustomed to the animals and the cautionary commands she received in their presence.

Lydia had a bowl of carrots beside her on the deck. She and Tim tossed several to the bull. He stepped forward to crunch the long roots with his powerful jaws.

"Look, Mom, he has a carrot sticking out under his nose. He almost looks like the snowmen we make at Christmas," Tim whispered.

"There he goes. He's heading back to the woods," Lydia said.

"Bye, ole fellow. We'll see you again next year. Stay safe and take care of Daddy," Tim shouted to the big bull.

The bull again walked up the path and turned before he entered the firs to look back at the mother, her son, and the dog on the deck. Dixie now stood and gave a quiet woof within her throat.

"You know Tim, it is really strange that he comes every year at this time and that he will eat the carrots we throw to him. Most wild animals won't come that close to people, and especially one so old and wise as this one."

"He comes from God and he knows we won't hurt him. I love the elk, don't you, Mom?" Tim asked.

"Yes, I do love that ole bull. I love what he means to us both and I'm very glad to see him every year. He reminds me of your Daddy and that he's in heaven. Let's pray and thank God for sending the bull to us again."

The two bowed their heads and offered their thanks.

They raised their heads and Tim's voice rang out toward the mountain. "Bye, old friend. Come again next year. We gotta go back to school. We'll be back next summer. Thanks for coming to see us." His voice echoed for a moment and then, all was very quiet. Tim, Lydia, and Dixie listened, but no sounds came.

Later, Reverend Jeff Boyd came alone to their home between the hunting season and Christmas.

During one of the busiest seasons of the year, he needed a reprieve from active duty. It always turned into a time of remembrance of his family and he couldn't help mourning his loss in his own private manner. God renewed his spiritual strength in time to carry him through Christmas without his wife and daughter.

When he called Archie, their conversation continued, "Don't bother to prepare the cabin. I can do it, but tell me how you put the anti-freeze back into the pipes so I can do that after my stay is complete."

Archie smiled, "I'll come show you how but you don't need to winterize the cabin again. Lydia, Tim, and Dixie will be here over part of Christmas, so I think I'll keep the auxiliary heat on for them. We won't need to fully winterize this time. I will tell you how, in case you need to leave quickly. Sometimes Vera and I are gone for a short time between Thanksgiving and Christmas, but this year, we plan to stick around."

Another Visit, Another Gift of Appreciation

When the Thayers returned for Christmas, there was a lovely rustic nativity scene where gifts had sat at other times. Again, an ivory envelope was tucked under the edge. His note read:

This scene so resembled your home, I made me a little homesick to see it again.

Somehow I feel that is the way heaven will seem for us. I already grow homesick, or perhaps it is the time of year when one should be spending time with our family. I know that neither of us have all of our family with us. It can be a lonely time, if we let it. I have my congregation and I've been invited to spend Christmas with some friends, but still. . . I know you understand, as you and your son also suffered a loss similar to mine.

I am reminded of the song lyrics which includes: "This world is not my home, I'm only passing through," but what a lovely earth our Lord has given us. Your home makes that so obvious to me when I'm there. Thank you again for the visit I had early this winter.

I'm sure by the time you see this, you are celebrating Christmas with your wonderful little man. Give him a hug for me and tell him he is a very fortunate young man to have such a lovely mountain cabin to share with his mom.

I didn't see your bull elk this year. Archie has told me about him, but I did see others. There were many cows and big calves roaming around during my latest visit. I always manage to see a great number of wild animals while I'm staying in your home. There were deer, I saw a lynx one day, cardinals, and magpies. One scolded me when I ventured onto your deck. It declared some sort of truce when I placed bread crumbs on the deck rail. It consented to partake of a portion of my humble meal.

You know the local animals better than I, so I won't go on.

Have a Blessed Christmas and wonderful New Year.

Your Unmet Friend,
Jeff Boyd

P.S.

I have become fascinated by the whole story of the elk's appearances each season at dawn on the day after hunting season. I realize it is a long while until the hunting season, but may I come see your elk this next fall and meet you and Tim?

Somehow I feel that I already know you, but I don't want to intrude, so I will understand if you don't wish for me to be present at your special time. Let me know and I'll plan thusly. Again my address is on the envelope, reply as to your answer.

Thank you again for the use of your home. It still brings such peace to my soul.

"Mom, let's do write him," Tim said.

Lydia answered, "We won't need to write for a bit. It's nearly ten months before that time, but we'll write him sometime this summer, if you want. I'll tell Archie he's coming, so he and Vera won't worry about us. They know it's okay for Pastor Jeff to be here at other times and they'll help see all goes well, " Lydia replied.

Consideration

Being considerate, Jeff again asked if they were sure it was okay for him to come visit their home at the end of the hunting season.

Lydia wrote to their minister friend.

I feel I should pay you to stay at our home each year as you repair and get things shipshape. Each of your accomplishments would cost me a bundle, should I hire a contractor. We can't thank you enough, but please don't feel you must work all the time you are there. You pay your way without doing my tasks.

Thank you so much for the Nativity set. You certainly don't need to leave us a gift each time you come, but this is quite appealing. It does fit well in the cabin.

> *Thank you again.*
> *We remain respectfully,*
> *Timmy and Lydia Thayer*

He replied:
Dear Mrs. Thayer,

As to my visit last time. It is very therapeutic for me to do some work amongst my leisure when I'm at your home. It costs me a whole lot less than psychiatric counseling, so don't feel I am over working.

I enjoy it immensely and if I had the time, I'd like to do a great deal more. Thank you again and please don't feel badly about me working on my vacation. Believe me, I'm not doing anything I don't wish to. However, if I am overstepping and doing something you dislike, please let me know and I can quickly undo the damage.

Again, my address is on this envelope if you care to reply on the cabin rental, or answer my question about the elk and the fall visit.

If your answer is no, don't worry, I will understand. I

*know this is a very special time for Tim and you, and I don't
wish to intrude or wear out my welcome.*
    Thank you again and God Bless.

                                        Sincerely, Jeff Boyd

    When Lydia finished reading the letter to Tim, he
studied his mother.
    "What should I tell him, Tim? Do you still want him
to come? Lydia asked.
    "It would be okay with me. What do you think,
Mom?" Tim asked.
    "I think it would be fine. I'd like to meet him.
Everything he does seems to be considerate and kind. He
won't stay long, so perhaps it would be okay. We'll tell
Archie and Vera he can come up that one morning. If we
don't want him to come anymore, we don't need to."
    "Let's write him a letter, Mom, and tell him he can
come. I know he'd like to meet Dixie too."
    "We'll send back his card. Next hunting season is still
a long ways away, so it may not work out for any of us by
then. We'll let him know he can come, but then make further
arrangements closer to time. We've got the whole summer to
come and enjoy our mountain again before fall arrives," she
said.
    "I wish it was now, but I don't want to miss out on all
the things before that time," Tim said.
    "Yes, we've got spring and summer before we even
think about it all, and you know that before our Messenger
comes again, you'll have school," she said.
    "Yuck, why did you mention that?" Tim asked.
    Lydia laughed. "Because it's true and you know you

really like school. Dixie even likes school. I do too, most of
the time."

Lydia and Tim spent many winter nights going back over their family videos of when Scott was still with them.

"It's easier, Mom. I used to be sad," Tim said.

"I think Dixie helped us both," Lydia said.

"She did. I love her," Tim said. He lay his head on Dixie's side. He turned over and hugged her.

'She's so neat. Dixie, you're so neat."

The dog licked his face. Tim wrestled her to the floor and lay on her.

"Gottcha, I win!" he yelled.

Lydia looked at the pair. "Tim, she looks like she's smiling. Look at her face," Lydia said.

Tim reared up. "She's happy. Me too," he said.

"Me too," Lydia said.

At Easter, Lydia wrote Pastor Jeff to tell him to go ahead with his plans for the close of the hunting season the next fall.

She gave him the dates for their visit at the cabin.

During their summer on Scott's Mountain, Pawpaw, Mawmaw, and the Grandparents Thayer all spent some of the summer with Tim and Lydia. Both sets of parents were still vigorous and able to keep up with some of Tim's adventures. Both sets of grandparents taught him some of the things they had taught Scott or Lydia as children.

Lydia's sister brought her husband and brood for a couple of long weekends.

Before they left the cabin at the end of summer, Lydia made plans with Tim.

"We'll stop to tell Archie and Vera, that Pastor Jeff will come for the end of the hunting season to meet us and to try to see our Messenger. That way, Archie and Vera won't worry about us. They know it's okay for Pastor Jeff to be here at other times and they'll help see all goes well," Lydia continued with their plans. "He'll stay with them, so they will know when he comes up to see us." Lydia didn't want to voice any anxiety to Tim. *I'll arrange for a signal to Archie and Vera, if the Reverend stays too late, Archie will come and check on us.*

Another Hunting Season

They made plans for their fall visit.

"Tim, we'll take off two days from school and go up. We can't be disappointed if the elk doesn't come. If he's just a wild animal, he will do this own thing and if he's a messenger from God, one of these days, we won't need him to remind us of Daddy anymore. If God is sending him, God could send us something else to keep us going." Lydia said. "We have to remember that the elk is very old. Animals don't live forever."

The little family arrived two evenings before the last day of the season. They were too late to more than shine a light around the yard and Dixie made a run around the perimeter. They walked inside, checked out the cabin and placed a few items from the cooler into the refrigerator.

The first morning they rose early and hiked to Scott's memorial site.

Despite the fact the minister wasn't going to be their live-in guest, they nervously prepared their home for a visitor.

Late that afternoon, Lydia baked a blueberry coffee cake and placed it in a cake saver at the center of their dining room table, along with silver, plates and napkins.

"I think I'll put a pot of coffee on the timer. Tim, do you want some cocoa in the morning?" Mom asked.

As the sun lowered, they went to the deck to watch the sunset.

Dixie lay between Lydia and Tim.

"Mom, it's so quiet here. I had forgotten until we got out here last night. Towns have too much noise. It makes us forget about the sounds of the mountain," Tim said.

"Yes, isn't it heavenly? I love it here," Lydia stretched.

"Me, too," Tim said, "I want to get up early, so I'll take Dixie and go on to bed."

"That's a very good idea. Think I'll drink a cup of chamomile tea and hit the sack too. We've had a very busy week and today was even more so. I'll come check on you and Dixie when you get settled in," Lydia said.

"Okay, Mom. Let's go Dixie, race you up the stairs!" Tim hollered.

"You'll both have to be quieter in the morning or you'll scare all the animals on our side of the mountain," Lydia laughed.

Finally dawn advanced on the appointed day after the close of the elk season.

Tim crept into his mother's room.

"Mom, I can't sleep. I think I'll go out on the deck," Tim whispered.

"Are you dressed?" Lydia asked.

"Yeah, I've got on my jeans and flannel shirt like Daddy's. My hiking boots too," Tim replied.

Lydia yawned, "I can't sleep either. I'll put on my warmer clothes, my coat, and be right out," Mom replied. "Wrap up and take a blanket."

Dixie padded along behind Tim and she heard the door snick shut. *They are being quiet.*

Tim looked out over Scott's Mountain, then sat down in his usual chair. He wrapped his fleecy blanket around his legs and called Dixie to his side.

"Down girl. Remember we have to be very quiet to see animals come from the mountain."

Dixie flopped beside him.

"Quiet, don't make so much noise," he cautioned.

After several minutes, Dixie turned her head and rumbled in her throat.

Tim looked toward the path and saw a shadow. Footsteps rasped on the rocky trail.

"It's okay, Dixie, it's Pastor Jeff coming to watch for God's Messenger too. He wants to see it for himself."

When the man arrived at the steps, he quietly spoke, "I'm Jeff Boyd, is it okay if I come up?"

"I'm Tim Thayer and this is Dixie. She's friendly. I've already told her you're okay. Here's a chair," Tim said.

"Where's your mom?" Pastor Jeff asked.

"She'll be out in a minute. I got up before she did but she said she'd be out soon."

The two settled into their chairs and turned toward the trail up the mountain. They spoke very softly.

"I didn't know you had a dog. Tell me about her," Pastor Jeff said. He spoke softly.

"We found her with a broken leg and her owner fixed her up for us. She's ours now and I really love her. She's always good when she's with us. Did you have a dog when you were young?" Tim asked.

"I've had dogs most of my life. Dixie looks like a very fine dog. May I pet her?" he asked.

"Yeah, she's friendly. Just let her smell your hand and she'll be all right. She protects me, but I already told her it was okay," Tim said.

When Lydia was dressed, she slipped out the door. She saw two shadows seated in two of the chairs on the deck. She could not see the man's face, but she assumed it was their house guest from the past several occasions. The man rose to assist her out the door.

"I hope you don't mind, but I awakened early and walked up the mountain from Archie's." He spoke quietly.

"That's fine. I know you want to see if our messenger comes this year too," Lydia replied. "Would you like a cup of coffee while we wait?"

"That would be great. Do you need help?" he asked.

"No, it's already made, I'll get a couple of mugs. Do you need any additives for your coffee?" she asked.

"Black is fine," Pastor Jeff said. Normally, he used cream, but he knew it would be difficult to get out the door with more than the two mugs.

Lydia rose and quietly opened the door. She returned quickly with a mug in each hand. Jeff rose and held the door for her, then accepted his cup.

She set hers on the chair arm. "Just a minute," Lydia said.

She returned from inside with three fleecy blankets. She handed one to each of the guys.

Jeff had stayed standing.

Lydia sat back down in her chair and drew her blanket around herself.

He seated himself once she was down.

The three settled in their chairs. Tim dropped the end of one blanket over Dixie.

Each cuddled into the warmth of his own blanket. Dixie lay quietly between Tim and the stranger.

Emotions hummed with anticipation. The night sounds quieted, as the nocturnal animals settled for the day. Birds began to awaken and cheered the dawn.

Once their coffee was finished, both adults set their cups on the floor of the deck by their chairs.

They all focused on the top of the mountain, as the light began to creep up the other side and lightened the silhouette of their mountain.

"I'm a little jealous of my Dad," Tim commented.

"Why, Son?" Mom asked.

"He stays here all the time."

"Not really. He's in heaven and that is even more beautiful and peaceful than here," Lydia replied.

"Yeah, you're right, but at least Dad's earthly body stays on the mountain the year round," Tim corrected himself.

The pastor kept quiet and listened to his two companions. *They've come a long ways in the time I've known about them. Glad I'm finally getting to meet them. Tim will be a pre-teen before we know it. He is going to be a good man. His mom has done a fine job.*

"There's the sun," Tim spoke in hushed reverence."

"It is no wonder ancient peoples wanted to worship the sun," Pastor Jeff spoke softly. "It is a constant in our world, but someday, even that will end. The true Son will continue into infinity."

"It saddens me to know God's beautiful world will someday vanish. It has given us such joy," Lydia whispered.

"God knew we'd enjoy the world He created and He planned it that way. He has bigger plans for us, we just need to go along with them," Jeff said. "You know, I don't even think we'll miss earth when we're in heaven. Heaven will be so beautiful, it will put this to shame. This is our earthly home and we're only to be here for a short time," he said.

The three were soon caught up in the splendor of the sunrise and each became oblivious to the others.

Dixie's head snapped around and she looked toward the mountain path.

"There he is, Mom! On the path, he's coming," Tim exclaimed quietly.

Dixie jumped up. "Stay. Sorry, I scared you ole girl," Tim apologized. His attention turned back to the elk.

"You have better eyesight than mine. Where?" Mom asked.

"Where he always comes down, right by that huge pine tree with the broken top," Tim pointed.

"You're right, I can see him coming," Mom said.

"If he weren't moving, I'd never be able to see him. You are both more accustomed to seeing wildlife, I struggle to see them until they move," Jeff replied.

"Mom, let's be quiet now and see if he comes into the yard again. Do you have the carrots ready?" Tim asked.

"Yes, Son, they're right here in this bowl."

An expectant hush fell over the three as the stately bull advanced slowly toward the yard. He seemed focused on them where they sat in anticipation.

The big bull advanced toward the path into the yard. He came onto the lawn and moved toward the deck.

Tim threw the first carrot.

The elk surveyed the group on the deck for several moments. He appeared to look into the face of each of the humans on the deck. Then he lowered his head to nudge the carrot in his path. He daintily picked it up and ate it as he had in previous years.

Minutes passed while the threesome watched in silence. Each folded into their own thoughts.

Tears streamed unchecked down Lydia's face.

Jeff looked at her and then his tears also started, partly in sympathy, partly for his own loss.

Tim sat with his arm around Dixie's neck and his mouth open. His breath came in spurts. An observer could see the boy's excitement.

Tim spoke very softly to the bull, "Have you seen my Daddy? Is he okay?"

The elk turned to look directly at the boy. No sound passed between the two, but Tim sighed. He appeared to have a satisfactory answer. Dixie whined and nuzzled his free hand.

Pastor Jeff cast up a prayer with his eyes on the elk. *Don't let them worship this elk, but the one who sent him. Thank you God for the sign that has helped to heal their hearts. Thank you for my healing as well. I pray blessings on this little family and I pray they can continue to move on with their lives. Keep the memories of our loved ones close, not in a crippling way, but in a good way. Let us carry on their good works and traits. Help us all when this bull ceases to appear on the mountain. If he's truly an animal, that time won't be much longer. Give us strength when he no longer appears. Help us to no longer need his appearance each year. In your Son's name, Amen.*

Everyone held their breath.

Tim tossed another carrot. The bull looked at it, nibbled and then dropped the carrot on the path.

He gazed at the three, seemed to bow his head, then turned and ambled back up the mountain. He lowered his antlers when he went under the low hanging branches.

When he reached the top, he appeared, turned toward them, then melted into the rising fireball of the sun.

The three waited, but when the sun cleared the tallest trees on the mountain top, the bull was no longer visible.

All were silent for several moments.

Tim and Dixie rose.

"That was awesome. He's bigger every year. Did you see, Mom, did you see?" Tim whispered.

"Yes, Tim, I did see him again. He is really something else and he never ceases to amaze me when he comes to us each year. I can't explain it, but I always feel better after he's been here," Lydia said.

She rose, picked up the mugs from the floor, and stepped toward the door, "Reverend, come in for coffee, if you like."

"I'd like to sit out here for a few minutes," Pastor Jeff said in a muffled voice, still moved by recent happenings. "I need to sort out my feelings on all that has happened here today." He rubbed his hand over his face to wipe away the evidence of his tears.

Lydia looked back and could see him with his head bowed.

Wonder what is going through his mind?

"Mom, can I take Dixie for a walk?" Tim asked.

"Yes, just stay in the yard, so we know where you are," she replied.

"Mom, I forgot to tell him good-by this time," Tim whispered.

"That's okay, the elk may not understand people talk, but God knows what is in your heart," she said.

Dixie and Tim scrambled down the steps and out into the lawn. They made the circuit inside the fence. Dixie checked the night scents and then the pair returned to the deck and tiptoed past Jeff and into the house.

Lydia moved toward the kitchen to prepare for their guest.

Tim and Dixie came in. He broke into her thoughts, "Can I eat?"

"What would you like? I have the blueberry coffee cake," she said.

"I'd like that and a glass of milk. Is Pastor Jeff coming in?" he asked.

I don't know, Son, but if he does, he can join us at the table. He may want to talk to God and then be quiet, so we'll have to wait and see," she said.

"I'm going to get myself some coffee, but I won't turn on the kitchen light, just in case he wants privacy. You and Dixie be quiet and I'll be right back. I think I'll have some cake with you too," she said.

As she returned, Pastor Jeff tapped on the door. His face still held evidence of his recent emotion.

Lydia directed him toward a chair at the dining room table. He moved to stand holding on to the back of the chair. He turned toward the little family.

"I've never seen anything like that and I have seen miracles before. It is truly amazing. I feel very blessed to have been able to be here with you. I think it is the same elk that came to me when I first came here so broken. I needed something then and I think God gave it to me through this animal. Thank you, Lord, " Pastor Jeff breathed.

Lydia spoke, "Pastor, would you offer a prayer for us all?" She stood with her arm around Tim. He leaned against her with his hand on Dixie's head.

"Certainly."

" Dear Father, we thank you for the blessing you have bestowed upon us. We have no words to express our thoughts and feelings at this amazing event. You know all that. You read our minds and hearts, but we feel we must offer an expression of our thanks and joy. You give encouragement constantly and we stay busy, we choose to overlook and ignore it. Forgive us for our blindness. Open our eyes to the everyday occurrences of your creation.

"Bless this family and give them comfort and peace as they come each year for a return of your message to them. May we all share that blessing with others in the message from your Holy Word.

"Be with us, guide us and protect us each day as we go about our daily activities and during the travel to and from this place.

"Again, we thank You in the name of your Son, Jesus Christ. Amen."

"Amen," Lydia breathed.

"Amen," Tim added.

"Pastor, would you like more coffee?" Lydia asked.

"Please." Jeff cleared his throat.

"I have a blueberry coffee cake on the table. Tim already has his milk and is getting ready to tank up. Go join him and I'll be right there," she added.

Jeff had pulled out a chair next to Tim when she brought his coffee. She set the cup down at his place and turned to her chair.

Jeff reached to pull out her chair for her and then seated her.

Tim looked at him and then at his mom.

"Well, what did you think of our Messenger?" Tim asked.

"He was awesome. He gets bigger every year. I saw him a few times, but then didn't the last time I was here. He is bigger than before," Jeff commented.

"I love him," Tim said.

"And you have a mighty fine dog here too. Do you two have a good time together?" Jeff asked.

"You should have seen us when we played in Mom's raked leaves. She buried us and we exploded the whole pile," Tim exclaimed.

Jeff looked over at Lydia, then back to Tim, "That sounds like fun. I used to like to play in the leaves at our house too. We lived in Vermont and had lots of leaves," Jeff explained.

"What color were your leaves?" Tim asked.

"Mostly the trees were maple, so they were red, gold, and yellow. Vermont has some of the most colorful leaves, but I like your fir and aspen in the fall. They are hard to beat."

"Did you see the aspens whirling in the fall? I like those best. Daddy used to say they looked like gold and red quarters quivering in the breeze," Tim explained.

Lydia cut the cake. She placed hers and Jeff's on plates and passed the plate to him. She lifted her first bite to her mouth.

She listened quietly to the conversation between her son and their new acquaintance. Pastor Jeff interacted with her son.

She felt a stab to her heart to see Tim with a man the age of his father.

Timmy has missed so much. I need to find him a mentor who he can relate to. He needs to do male things. He's just a little boy, but I'll soon lose him when he outgrows a mommy and becomes a teen. I wish my father lived closer. He's a good role model and he loves Tim.

Oh, how I miss my husband!

She looked down, her eyes welled. To mask her emotion, she rose to get the coffee pot.

* * *

The next day, Pastor Jeff walked to their cabin. He asked another favor before he left.

"If you don't mind, I'd like to stay on a few days after you leave. If that's all right? I'll be down at Archie's and Vera's until you are ready to go."

"I can't thank you enough for my chance to see your Messenger from God. I'll never forget this experience and what it meant to me," he said.

He turned to the family group. "Thank you, for allowing me in on the visit."

He shook each of the family's hands, patted Dixie on the head, turned away and walked down the trail.

Tim watched him go. He looked at his mother, "Can Pastor Jeff come back tonight?"

Lydia was flustered. *I do want him to come.*

"I think that's a good idea," Lydia said. "You can run down and ask him to come back for a minute."

Tim and Dixie took off down the trail. "Pastor Jeff, Pastor Jeff. Wait up," Tim yelled.

Pastor Jeff stopped and looked back at the pair.

Tim skidded on a rock and Jeff reached to save the boy a fall.

"Whoa there, you're about to take a tumble!" He said.

"Can you come back to dinner tonight? Mom and I want you to," the boy asked.

"Let's go talk to Mom and see what she has in mind." Jeff put his hand on Tim's head and turned him toward the cabin. He didn't remove his hand until they climbed the steps where Lydia waited. Jeff thought she seemed flustered.

"Don't feel obligated to entertain me," he said.

"We really would like to get to know you better. We won't go to any trouble. I have a roast for the slow cooker, so whether there are two or three, it won't make any difference," Lydia said.

"Okay, I'd like that, but promise me you won't go to a lot of trouble," Jeff said. "I cook for myself, sort of, and I know how much time and effort a minor meal can take."

"It gets dark early now, why don't you come to eat about five," Lydia said. "That way, you will have some light at least one-way."

"Five, it is. Thank you very much. I'll be seeing you all later," he turned again. "Bye, for now."

Lydia and Tim both spoke at once, "Bye."

They stepped into the house and Tim danced a jig. "He's coming, he's coming. I can't wait!"

"I didn't realize you wanted him to come so badly, or we could have talked about it before," Lydia said.

"I didn't know until this morning, but I had a good time with him. I wanted to see him again," Tim replied.

"Well, let's get ready. Go be sure your bed is made and your things arranged neatly," she said.

"Oh, I didn't do that this morning. I got up too early," he said. Tim scooted up the stairs to his bedroom. She could hear him banging things around.

Evening

Jeff arrived at four forty-five.

Tim ran to meet him with his basketball in his hands.

"Good evening, have you both recovered from the early morning?" He greeted Tim, then Lydia.

"It was exhilarating. I don't think we've stopped since you left," Lydia replied.

"Is there anything you wish me to do to help you, Mrs. Thayer?" he asked.

"No, it's under control. You and Tim get acquainted and I'll be out in a few minutes," she said.

"Tim, you've got your basketball. Do you want to shoot a few hoops?" Pastor Jeff asked.

"I'd really like to. You gotta watch Dixie though, she gets excited and might trip you. I'll have her down, and stay at the edge of the court, because we men might get a little rough for her. Come, Dixie. Down, stay." Tim positioned his dog as an excited spectator.

She whined, but stayed put when Tim bounced the ball toward Pastor Jeff.

It didn't take long for Tim to see Pastor Jeff knew what he was doing.

Soon, Lydia came from the cabin and watched the two. She could see Dixie wiggle on the stay.

Dixie looked at Tim for her release. They had always made a policy of having her obey the last one who gave a command.

Tim held the basketball."Okay, Dixie," he called.

She ran onto the court, then Lydia called to her. "Come, Dixie."

When the guys tired with their playing, they came toward the deck for a drink.

Lydia had the food on the picnic table and the group seated themselves.

Tim was so excited he could hardly think of eating.

"Mom, did you see Pastor Jeff make that lay-up, he's as good as Michael Jordan. Or those dribbles he made. He showed me how to dribble through his legs. I even made two baskets. Wow, that was fun!" Tim was beside himself.

In a few minutes, every play was noted, grace was said and the threesome dived into a picnic-style dinner of roast beef, potatoes, carrots, brown gravy and hot bread.

Lydia had laid out the sticks for marshmallows for dessert. Tim finished first and prepared his toasted to black crisp over the outdoor fireplace.

"Mrs. Thayer, how do you like your marshmallows?" Pastor Jeff asked.

"Browned on the outside, melted on the inside, but not burned or flamed," Lydia said.

Pastor Jeff browned a couple for Lydia and then prepared a stick full of burned ones for himself.

"Anyone wish for more?" he asked.

"I'm done, can't hold another bite," Tim said.

"I've had plenty, thanks. Those were just right, but I can't hold another bite either," Lydia said.

"Likewise for me too,"Pastor Jeff said.

They sat before the fire after they ate. The deck fireplace put out enough heat to keep them comfortable.

After three hours of continuous chatter, mostly between Tim and Pastor Jeff, Lydia rose.

"I need to get these cleared up. Tim, it's about your bedtime. I guess you'd better tell our guest good night and go get your PJ's on," she said.

Jeff rose quickly. "I'm very sorry, I enjoyed our conversation so much, I've totally forgotten the time. Please forgive me for keeping this young man up. I thank you for the wonderful experience you allowed me to share. I won't soon forget this whole day." He went on, " Thank you for the lovely dinner too. I don't know when I've enjoyed myself so much."

"Perhaps you'd like to come again after Sunday church services? We'll be preparing to leave later Sunday afternoon, but we could visit a little on the deck, if you'd like," she said. *Why did I say that?*

"I'd like that very much. I'd like to know each of you better. I seldom get treated as a person. Most people think of me as a pastor. It's a refreshing change to be with those who aren't in my congregation. I like the experience. Thank you."

"I'll fix a pot of chili in the slow cooker and you can eat with us. How about right after we return from church?" Lydia said.

"I would like that. Thank you very much. I'll be seeing you then," he turned toward Tim and Dixie.

"Tim, I'll be seeing you, your mom, and Dixie tomorrow. Maybe some day next summer, I can come to Archie's and take you fishing, if your mom says that is okay," Jeff said.

"Mom, could I?" Tim asked.

"We'll have to see nearer to time," Lydia seemed flustered.

Tim and Dixie made a quick perimeter check and were back up on the deck. He hugged his mom, turned to shake Jeff's hand and ran up the stairs with Dixie hot on his heels.

"I apologize, again. I seem to put my foot into my mouth when I'm with your family. I should have asked your permission before I mentioned anything to your son about fishing," Jeff said.

"It's a long time before summer and many things can happen by then. We'll see if a fishing expedition might be worked out when the time comes," she said. "Archie likes to fish, he might go along with the two of you. He can show you the best spots," she said.

"You're right. I understand you don't know me and might be reluctant to allow your son to go with me alone for an activity. You'd be welcome to come along, I didn't want to seem presumptuous in thinking that you might not enjoy fishing," Jeff said.

She smiled to soften her words. "I do like to fish, especially fly fishing in these cold waters. You'd better bring along some good waders, these streams come off snow and they freeze your feet if you go barefoot. I've tried it and I know," she said.

"Then if you don't mind, I'll get you and Tim a license for next summer and we'll give it a try. Do you have equipment, or do I need to get that?" he asked.

"Actually, we have enough equipment to outfit a whole crew for a fishing expedition. We even have some flies my husband and I tied. You'll be amazed at how lifelike they look. Some have even been used successfully in the past. I'll hunt out the ones I know work, and we'll see if we can get enough fish for a good meal out of the day's experience. We'll look forward to a fishing expedition next summer."

"By the way, how did you catch the trout you shared with Archie and Vera?" she asked.

He looked down, "I used a long tree branch, a little line and a stick for a cork. Primitive, but it worked for the few I caught."

"Can't beat that old-time equipment." She smiled. "We'll teach you to fly fish when you return."

Lydia got a faraway look. "It's the most beautiful fishing you'll ever see." She turned and looked into the night.

"I look forward to it. Thank you for a lovely evening. I'll see you at church Sunday and for lunch afterwards." he said.

"We'll be there," Lydia said.

"Good night and thank you again," Jeff turned toward the door.

Lydia followed and held the door for him.

"Don't forget to lock up after I get out," Jeff said.

"I'll do that and I'll also turn on the flood light so you can see part way down the trail toward Archie's. Do you need a flashlight?" she asked.

"No, I have a small one in my pocket. I'll make it fine. Thanks again and I pray good blessings on you and your family," he said.

"Same from us to you," she said. She flipped on the light as he walked to the steps leading down from the deck. She clicked the deadbolt on the door and turned to go up the stairs and tuck Tim into bed.

When she got to Tim's room, he was looking out the window as Jeff walked down the trail. Lydia watched Tim while he stared after the man. As Pastor Jeff reached the edge of the lighted area, he turned to wave at Tim. The boy returned his wave, then turned to pat Dixie.

Tim climbed into bed.

"You both better get some sleep so we can be up and out early in the morning. We've only got another day until we need to go back to school. Sleep tight. I love you, Son," she said and kissed him good night.

"Me too, Mom. I love you too," he turned on his side and tucked his hand under his face.

Lydia looked out his window one more time. Jeff was almost out of sight and she saw his little flashlight come on and bounce along the trail.

She looked back at Tim and turned toward the hallway to go down to her bedroom. She looked at Dixie and pointed her finger at the dog. "Take care of him."

Dixie's tail gave a thump on the floor and then she sighed and lay her head on her paws.

Lydia wagged her fingers and flipped off Tim's light. She had much to think about.

It bothered me to have some other man make my marshmallows for me. That was one of Scott's jobs.

On the Road to the City

After an afternoon of chili, then a mountain hike, Lydia and Tim prepared to leave. Pastor Jeff carried their baggage to the car.

Dixie and Tim galloped one last circuit of the yard. The next time Lydia looked out, they walked the top of the wall, Tim ahead, Dixie followed. The dog stepped carefully on the rugged tops of the mountain stones.

Already a winter chill filled the air, their down parkas felt delightfully cozy.

They gave Pastor Jeff a ride back to Archie and Vera's. He was going to take his belongings back to the cabin for a short stay.

Their farewells to everyone took a few minutes with hugs all around.

Everyone wished them well. They left Vera, Archie, and Pastor Jeff standing in the road waving. Tim turned his head and waved through the back glass.

On the road, Tim was quiet for a long while. Lydia thought he was asleep.

"Mom, I like Pastor Jeff. He seems like fun," the boy exclaimed.

"He did seem nice. I'm glad you enjoyed his visit." She changed the subject, "Wasn't the ole Messenger something else?"

"Awesome, he's always awesome. Dixie was nice too. She didn't bark at all," Tim said.

"She is a very good dog," Lydia agreed.

Tim was quiet again and Lydia mused to herself. *He did seem like a nice man. I've suspected he was from all the things he's done when he visited the cabin in the past couple of years. He's been most thoughtful. I imagine he's a good pastor. He seems very concerned about his congregation. He's good with kids, if his conversations with Tim are an example.*

I do wish he'd asked me before he mentioned a fishing trip to Tim. I want to be very sure of anyone who takes my son out for any reason. I think Jeff understood that, after he had already made the gesture. Surely that won't happen again. If he returns for that trip, I'll make certain Archie or I go along.

After their early winter visit to the cabin, she felt more lonely and restless than she had at any time since Scott's death.

Why am I dissatisfied with my life? For the past several years, we have adjusted and settled into our routine. Life has been good, not perfect, but satisfactory. Tim is healthy and happy. He loves Dixie and she's been a very good influence on all of us. She gives us a feeling of safely when she's with us. My work is satisfying. I have time to paint some scenes and portraits of my own interests, while Dixie entertains Tim in the backyard. He would never stay out that long by himself. It is great exercise for both of them and they both seem very happy. Tim never gives me any trouble. He's a lot like his Dad.

Oh, how I wish Scott could see his son now. He'd be so very proud. I think he'd be proud of us both. We've done very well in settling into a life he and I never planned for our family, but it is the best Tim and I can do, under the circumstances. God sent us Dixie at the right time. She filled a void in Tim's life and I've enjoyed her too.

Thank you Lord, for your care in all our times of trouble and in the good adjustments we've made. Thank you for my Tim. Thank you for life, prosperity, all the things you've given us. Thank you for good friends at work and for Archie and Vera. We are so grateful insurance provided in a way we were able to keep our home in the mountains. It has been our anchor on earth, while You and Scott have been our anchors from heaven. Thanks for providing for us and keeping us safe.

We praise You for your goodness. We love You. Thank You, Lord. In Jesus' name, Amen.

Over several weekends, Lydia tried to fill their leisure hours. She took Tim and Dixie to the local nursing home. The staff checked Dixie out as to temperament and ability to tolerate large numbers of people. After their clearance, the residents enjoyed having a dog visit.

They didn't see children often, so many were taken with Tim. Lydia was pleased to see him display kindness and genuine love for those in the home.

Despite their busy activities, she and Tim had a difficult time settling back into their routine.

Christmas at Home
Christmas Eve

After school closed for the Christmas and New Year's vacations, Lydia and Tim drove to see the grandparents and her sister first, then on to Scott's Mountain.

When Lydia opened the door to their cabin for their Christmas Vacation in their mountains, Tim and Dixie ran inside.

"Mom, look, there's a note on the table again."

"What does it say?" Mom asked.

"I can't read it very well, maybe you better read it for us," Tim replied. "I think it's from Pastor Jeff."

Lydia unfolded the note.

Dear Friends,

I hope you don't mind me calling you that, as I feel that I am better acquainted with both of you and that you are my friends. Anyone who can be so generous to share their lovely cabin and Messenger with me, must be newfound friends.

I left a gift for both of you this year. I hope you don't feel I am being presumptuous. If so, I apologize.

With the coziness of your home and the cold of the outside, I thought perhaps you could use some cocoa for the MAN of your house and some chocolate hazelnut and other coffee varieties for yourself as a special treat. You served me coffee on my last visit, so hope these suit your taste. When I put in my supplies, there is always a can of coffee in your freezer, so I assume that you or your guests can enjoy these coffees. If you don't like these flavors, perhaps your guests will.

There are some other items: pancake/waffle mix, biscotti, white chocolate cookies, and double chocolate hot cocoa, also raspberry and peach teas, if you prefer. I put these in the breakfast tray along with a floral mug for you with flowers like your painting on the bedside table. For your son, I included a mug with a magnificent elk. I had heard so much about YOUR Messenger Elk and in seeing him for myself, I thought Tim might like that. There are Christmas napkins, so you both can enjoy your treats in front of the fire, or even on the deck, if the weather is pleasant.

These items sounded good to me. My wife used to enjoy chocolate in any form, and coffee or tea on a cold night. I am assuming you might enjoy the same. If not, share the items with someone else and know they are for the enjoyment of whoever likes them.

I'm sure you can cook from the samples I've had in your home over my several visits. I don't mean to tread on your expertise, but please accept these items as a token of my appreciation for again sharing your home with me.

I had a wonderful and restful three days there. Each time I come, I marvel at God's creations in the forest, the animals, the trees, and the mountain. The more I look at your cabin, I see it was built with loving hands. You and your husband added many clever and thoughtful additions. An observer can see that each log was laid with care. Your deck

overlooking the lawn and the trees is a God-send for me. I
spend more time there than anywhere, but the fireplace in the
evening is a close second. I can sit and gaze into the fire for
hours.
Such peace settles over me when I'm inside or out.
The whole place offers me time with God and time for Him to
deal with me.
Each visit, I go away refreshed and ready to meet the
next challenges of my ministry. I wrote that wrong, it is His
Ministry and I pray I can allow it to remain so.
Thank you again and may you have a Blessed
Christmas and Happy New Year.
I hope you enjoy the goodies. I'll be thinking of you
both on some cold winter night and imagine you sipping
from your mugs before a blazing fire.
Sincerely,
Jeff

Later, Lydia and Tim strung their small white lights on
a tiny potted fir tree. It would go outside each night and when
they left, it would go into a hole by the side of their stone
wall, strung with berries and food for the wildlife during their
absence from the mountain.
"Mom, let's light our candles, turn on our tree lights,
and sit in the dark. I like to look at all the sparkle," Tim said.
"We can look out at the stars too." She went to her
husband's special window, "Did you notice the snow sparkles
where our lights shine through the window? It's too dry for a
snowman but it sure is pretty tonight."
"I wish he was here," Tim said.
She knew, but she had to ask, "Who?"
"Daddy."
"Me too, Buddy, me too. He wants us to be happy, so
let's get those lights off and I'll zap us some popcorn. We can

eat that and drink our hot cocoa by the tree lights," she added.

Tim turned out the overhead lights while she popped the corn in the microwave.

"Sit here, Mom, we can see the Christmas tree and the snow all at the same time."

Lydia noted Tim had Scott's cap on his knee.

"Let's open our gifts tonight," she said.

"Okay," Tim said.

Dixie caught their excitement and started barking.

"Okay, okay, hold your horses. Let me dig out your present first," he said. He handed her the first present and helped her unwrap the paper.

"Here, Dixie, here. It's a new dog bone in HUMONGOUS size. You won't be able to destroy that for a few days," he said.

The next morning, Lydia found Tim inside the closet that contained some of Scott's hunting clothes.

"What are you looking for, Tim?" she asked.

"I'm smelling Daddy's clothes," he said.

"Sometimes, I do too. I seem to think I can still smell your Daddy on his pillow," Lydia said.

"I like his camouflage hat and ski mask best. They smell more like him," Tim said.

Lydia picked up the mask. She held it at her nose. Immediate memory flooded back into her senses. She didn't speak for a moment.

"You're right. These have not been washed and they do smell like Daddy." She hugged Tim to her. She held the ski mask, while Tim held the cap.

Before they left, she and Tim folded Daddy's set of camouflage clothes carefully in tissue and laid them back into Tim's dresser drawer.

"One of these days, you may want to wear Daddy's

clothes. That would have made him very proud. He liked to take you out with him. The first time you went out in your little outfit, you were only three years old," she said. "I should have kept those cammies, but I gave the set to a little boy at church when they had a house fire."

"That's okay, Mom. I don't know if I remember going at three, but I do remember going with him sometimes. I remember we saw a lynx in the snow once. It was looking for food around a log. I remember when we trapped the turkeys," Tim said. Then he looked down. "That was about the time Daddy got sick." He sniffed.

"Yes, that was one of the last times he went out on official business for his job," she said.

"Did that little turkey set the next year?" Tim asked.

"The fellows said she did and she brought off five little ones," Lydia said.

"Daddy would have been happy to know they were able to track her and find out she was okay," Tim said.

"You're right, Daddy always tried to take care of the forest and the animals that live there. That was the task God gave him to do and he did a very good job of it. He took good care of us too. He'd have liked to have stayed with us, but his body hurt too much. Jesus knew that and took him home to live in heaven," she said.

"I want to see him someday," Tim said.

"You made a profession of faith in Jesus last winter at our other church. You asked Jesus into your heart to be your Savior then. You will see your Daddy one day. He'll be there waiting for you and he will probably greet you even before anyone knows you're gone," she said. "The Bible speaks of the twinkling of an eye and that's about a 100 millionth of a second, or something like that. A whole lot less time than we can even imagine."

"Wow, God really is fast!" Tim said.

"He's stronger than anyone or anything too," Lydia said.

Heading Toward Spring

Correspondence with Pastor Jeff picked up after they met him in the fall. Over the months, he revealed more and more about his personal life and his ministry.

At first, Lydia was reluctant to show vulnerability or to become too involved, but as time advanced, she found herself coming to know the man behind the gifts he had left in appreciation for the use of their mountain as his retreat.

Again, he requested to come to the mountain in the spring before school was out. He still didn't wish to interfere with their vacation time.

Lydia gave permission.

When they arrived at the cabin, they found a roast in the freezer with a note attached.

This is to provide the main dish, should our fishing expedition meet with failure. Love, Jeff

Tim crowed, "I am actually going fishing with men, instead of my mom, for a change. We'll get as dirty as we want and we won't be worried about washing our hands all the time!"

"I didn't know you minded that much?" Lydia said.

"I don't really mind, I know all about germs. We learned in science class, but men are different than ladies," he added.

"Son, God made both men and women and He said both are very good, but I'm sure you also notice they have different ways and actually all make a very good team when they work together. They're kind of like a puzzle, where one is weak, the other can fill in, but where that one is weak, the other fills in. It takes both of them to make a whole complete picture," Lydia said. "Not all men are good at fishing, and not all women are good at cooking. It takes all of us to get the job done. Men may be stronger to lift with their physical strength, but women have other abilities that even it all out. You'll learn a lot about men and women in the years to come," Lydia added. "You may find out Jeff is super clean too. You may be surprised."

She caught herself, *I'm preaching. I never want to do that. I want to lead Tim by example.* She hugged Tim to her.

"Mom, you may be surprised, he may like to get dirty too," Tim added. His eyes twinkled with mischief.

"You could be right, guess we'll find out soon enough," she said. "Uh, Tim, don't grow up too fast," she said.

Tim gave her an odd look.

"You don't have to understand, it's one of those things moms do. Okay?"

"Sure, Mom," he said. "One of those women things."

She ruffled his forelock and they smiled into each other's eyes.

*   *   *

Tim less frequently asked for Daddy Stories.

I mustn't let him forget, Lydia prompted herself. She carted out more of Scott's videos for them to view on weekends. Tim had his two birthday ones nearly memorized.

After Tim looked at the parents at their school program, he asked his mother, "Did Daddy ask you to marry him?"

"Yes, he took me for a canoe ride. We got out into the middle of the lake and Daddy pretended to drop his paddle. He knelt in the floor of the canoe and said, "I'm going to have to ask you to marry me, because we're stuck here for the rest of our lives."

Tim laughed. "Oh, Mom, you weren't stuck!"

"I was a little scared and happy too, so I said, 'Are you sure?' He looked at me and said, 'Yes, I am sure I love you,'" she said.

"What did you say?" Tim asked.

"I said, Yes, I will marry you, but you better find a way to get us back to shore or I am going to be very mad at you. This water is way too cold for a swim tonight. Daddy laughed and brought the paddle out from under the seat. He tried to fool me. Then Daddy said, 'And the water in the bottom of this canoe is very cold, so can I have your answer soon. My wet knee has frozen to the metal.'"

"Then what?" Tim asked.

"We paddled back to shore and he fished an engagement ring out of the watch pocket of his jeans. He said he was afraid to give it to me on the lake, afraid we'd drop it, or I'd be upset and throw it into the water. He also said it wasn't totally paid for and he didn't want to be feeding a dead horse," she said.

Tim had a very worried expression, "You can't feed a dead horse, it can't eat!"

"Tim, it had nothing to do with a dead horse, that's a saying people use when they mean they are paying for something that is already gone. If we had lost the ring, it would have been gone and Daddy would still have had to pay the jeweler for it," Lydia said.

"Would he have gotten you another one?" Tim asked.

"I think he would have. We loved each other very much by that time, but neither of us had much money. Remember we were both in college and trying to pay for that, plus our own living expenses. We didn't have much to spare. It would have been very hard for Daddy to buy that ring and another one too. I've still got my rings on. He had a wedding band for me, to go with the diamond. It came as a set. We got a wedding band for him that looked almost like mine," she added.

"But Daddy's was bigger," Tim smirked.

"You're kidding? Yes, we could put mine inside his and it didn't touch. I have Scott's in my jewelry box. It will be yours one day," Lydia said. "We were both very proud of those rings. I still wear mine, but would you mind if I put away my wedding ring? Daddy's gone and I'm not married, even though I wish he was still here and we were still married. I think I'd like to wear my diamond on my other hand now, if it is okay with you," Mom said.

"Would it mean you don't love Daddy anymore?"he asked.

"I still love your Daddy very much. I would take him back in a second, if he were here, but we know he's with Jesus and he can't come back, even if he wants to. I know he would want to be with us, but his body was so sick, we couldn't ask him to stay and hurt any longer. It's hard to understand that a man who seemed so healthy could actually get something that bad," Lydia said.

"Will I get sick, like Daddy did?" he asked.

"I don't think so, but best of all, we know God is with us and no matter what, we'll be okay. We know signs to watch for and we go to the doctor to be checked out. We would know much sooner and the doctors would be able to help us. We were so busy and happy with Daddy, we didn't realize he had a problem until it was too late. We weren't expecting anything like that to come along. God gives us our bodies and He expects us to take care of them, just like Daddy tried to take care of the forest, the animals that live here, the water, and the land. That's called stewardship. God has given us the job of being a steward of His creation. He expects us to act responsibly when we use what He has given us. Daddy was very serious about taking good care of God's creation. That's why he was so careful when he hunted, or when we used any of the things the land provides."

"And when we made campfires," Tim added.

"Yes," Lydia said.

"Mom, let's go put your ring in the box, and can I see Daddy's?" he asked.

"Sure," she put her hand on his head and turned him toward her bedroom.

He carried her wedding ring, almost reverently, in the palm of his hand.

She opened her drawer, retrieved the jewelry box and handed it to her son.

Tim tested to see if her ring would go inside his Daddy's. He placed both on his own small finger. Then he lay the two together in tissue paper, folded it over, and lay them in her jewelry box. He snapped the lid shut and put it back in her drawer.

Lydia had to look away.

Legalities

After school one day, Lydia found a letter in their mailbox from a law firm.

One of the partners requested a meeting with her. The lawyer proposed to meet her at her home, or his office in a nearby town.

Lydia called the designated number.

"This is Lydia Thayer, I understand one of the partners in your firm wishes to meet with me. Could I ask how this concerns me?"

The receptionist rustled some papers.

"I'm afraid I'm not at liberty to relay that information. You'll have to take that up with one of the partners."

"I will come to the office, give me a time on Thursday. It will need to be after school. I have a son and can't leave him until then," she indicated.

Lydia was nervous when she left Tim with Carmen, her fellow teacher, who lived nearby.

"I won't be long. I can't imagine what they want. It's been a long time. All the loose ends have been tied up from Scott's estate. He had everything well prepared for us," Lydia told her friend.

"It looks like they could have indicated what they wished to see you about. That's not very considerate of them to worry you," Carmen said.

"Well, I need to go get this over with. You have my cell phone, if you need anything," Lydia said.

Carmen gave her a hug.

"I've got some things for Tim and I to do. No hurry, we'll have fun. I also have a pizza in the frig if you're late."

Lydia was very nervous when she entered the law firm's swank building. She was directed into the plush office of Jones, Jones and, Bell. The receptionist sent her to the third floor and an even more plush office.

Lydia shivered. *I don't like this place for some reason, I feel very uncomfortable here. It is pretty but there's not really any warmth, just expensive stuff.*

A suave young man stepped through one of the doors.

"Ms Thayer, come on in," he said.

Lydia seated herself before his desk.

"I am one of the Jones in the name of the firm. I won't take much of your time. Did you know the University and the Forestry Service could be responsible for the early death of your husband?" he stated.

Lydia reeled in shock. "What do you mean? He died from lung and other cancers, I've heard nothing about any liability from any source," she stuttered.

"It is possible they contaminated some of the area where your husband and others worked planting trees the summer of 1998. It is the Valley Site on the Forest Ridge property. If that contamination can be proven, you could collect a huge amount of compensation from both institutions," he said.

"What proof do you have that either was at fault?" she asked.

"During some of the research, pollutants were accidentally released into one of the forest campus reservoirs. Scott and others worked in that area for an entire summer. There have been some other casualties, but none have died. It appears all the others will recover, with time. Scott was the youngest and being the most serious loss, his heirs could collect the most," the lawyer stated. "We wish to represent you in this case. Since we've already worked with some of the others, we feel certain of a good settlement for you and your son. Your case would vastly strengthen the other cases."

Lydia took a breath to still her trembling.

"We miss my husband and my son's father, but Scott loved the University and the forestry service. His folks work for the University. His life was tied up with it. He'd be appalled if either had to pay compensation for his death. He'd be upset if any of the programs had to be cut due to legal ramifications," she said.

She continued, "I don't wish to pursue this any further. My son and I have adjusted to our loss and we don't want to cause anymore problems or bring up issues that would cause either of the organizations problems," she arose. "A suit would not bring back Scott. He loved that University, I do too, and I don't wish to pursue a suit against our alma mater. If they did something wrong, it was not intentional. If they are at fault, I'm sure they will, and have investigated. They are a research institution and will get to the bottom of it. Let's let it rest, as far as we're concerned, it is done," she said. She rose from her chair.

"Ms Thayer, you should consider these issues. These entities owe you and your son for your loss. We'd be assured of a tidy sum," the lawyer said. "You owe it to your son, for his future."

Lydia was angered.

"I know about legal fees and you would collect about as much as we would. I don't want to associate with blood money. I can't speak for the others, but forget our case, we've moved on and I don't want us to go back," Lydia picked up her purse from her chair and marched toward the door.

"Ms Thayer, you'll be sorry!" The lawyer spoke harshly.

"No, I won't. I live with myself and I want to be able to have a clear conscience and feel good about myself for my own and my son's sakes. As far as we're concerned, it is over and done. Good day, Mr. Jones!"

She walked out of the office. She didn't take the elevator. *I don't want to see anyone in this building. I think I'm going to be sick!* She ducked into the closest stairwell. She put her forehead against the cold block wall.

A door snicked closed. She heard voices in the hall. She could hear the men in a heated discussion.

"A no-go, you say?"

"It would require a lot of pressure, but I'm not confident we'd get her to acquiesce even then. I never figured on a do-gooder or someone with ethics. Everyone wants easy money now."

The voices passed down the hall.

Get out of here, screamed in Lydia's head. She took the stairs to the lobby. Looked through the crack in the stairwell door, and left the building. She entered her car and fled the lot on squealing tires.

I can't pick up Tim now. I'm too upset. I need to get out and walk to settle my nerves.

She pulled into the nearest convenience store parking lot and punched in Carmen's phone number.

"Carmen, I can't come for about a half hour. Will that work?" she asked.

"Lydia, are you all right? You don't sound like yourself," Carmen asked.

"I'll be okay in a bit, but I need to walk to clear my head. I don't want Tim to see me upset. I'll be along as soon as I can get hold of myself. It isn't something I can talk about right now, but I'll tell you when I see you. Is it okay if Tim stays a little longer?" she asked.

"Sure, what are friends for? I'll send up a little prayer. Be careful," Carmen said.

Lydia pulled into a park where children played on the swing set. *I can see adults, I'll feel safe here.*

She walked, some might have said she stomped in her sensible teacher shoes.

After a half hour, she made a resolution to herself.

I will never again think of that lawyer's proposal. After the walk around the perimeter, she could not leave it there. *What if others were exposed or would be exposed? I'd never forgive myself if I allowed a pollutant to remain in the water or in the ground. It could cause others to suffer as Scott and we have. I've got to tell someone and get it checked out. If there is something that will damage anyone or the environment, I owe it to Scott and anyone who might be involved.*

I don't want to hurt the university, I don't want any money, I just want everyone to be safe.

Oh, God, help me to find the right person to help me get to the bottom of this.

She went to a pay phone near the lawyer's office.

"Joseph, this is Lydia Thayer," she said.

"Lydia, I've been meaning to call you. How are you and Tim doing?" he asked.

"We're fine. Joseph, I don't have a lot of time, but could you do me a favor? Let me explain before you agree. I need some soil and water tested, but it has to be in strictest confidence. Regardless of what occurs, can you recommend someone?" she asked.

"Uh, sure. Lydia, you are worrying me. Spill it, so I'll know what you're getting in to," he said.

"I've got to talk to someone in a research department who will be neutral in his findings. They will have to want what is best for everyone, regardless of where the chips might fall," she said.

"Let me think a bit. It depends a little on what kind of tests you need run," he stated.

Lydia put a hand to her forehead. "I think water and soil would do it," she said.

Joseph got quiet. In a moment he said, "If this involves the University, maybe you'd better use an independent lab. Most of the research teams at the University have specific projects. I'm not sure they'd have time to run what I think you might be aiming for."

"Have you heard rumors, or are you guessing?" Lydia asked.

"There's always rumors, campus politics and all, you know. I'm sure Scott mentioned some with his Dad working there."

"I don't want to hurt anyone or put them on the spot in their job. Probably an outside team would be the best,. Do you have any suggestions?" Lydia asked.

"I'll get back to you," Joseph said.

Lydia was torn. *I don't want to do this. I don't want to stir up any trouble for the University, but I need to protect others, the animals, that whole area. If it had a problem, something dangerous may still be there.*

It needs to be cleaned up. Oh, God, am I doing the right thing?

Several days passed before Joseph returned her call. "I can't talk but a moment, but try Industrial and Environmental Research Company, out of Colorado Springs. They work with environmental problems and are reported to be the best in the nation. Hope you find what you need. Uh, gotta go. I'll be seeing you around." He hung up abruptly.

Lydia called the company to make a brief explanation of her problem. She did not reveal where the pollution might have occurred.

"Hello, I am Lydia Thayer. Does your company check out soil and water pollution which might have caused some health issues and even possible death?"

The lab's receptionist put Lydia through to one of the research labs.

She again explained her situation.

"We do those kinds of tests. You can bring the samples here, but those would be only preliminary tests. If we found any pollutants, we would need to collect our own samples, under strict conditions, and then test those in the lab here. There are a few tests, that require we go to a more advanced lab for analysis. If you are serious about the testing, you can bring the preliminary samples and meet with us sometime this next week. I am about ready to start a new project, but could work your tests in between the two projects," the research technician stated.

She hesitated. *I feel like I've been swimming*

underwater too long. My head is whirling.

"Can I call you back in a few hours? I need to think a little bit about how I am going to accomplish all this. The samples are a distance away and it is winter time. I'm not sure if I can work out the logistics of retrieval and then delivery to you in that short a time. I'm not sure I can manage it by next week. Did you have a certain day you had in mind for me to bring the samples?" she asked.

"I was thinking of Thursday. I am to receive the samples I need for my next project on the following Monday, so I need to start that immediately. It might be up in the day Monday, for the delivery time, but probably not later than noon. If I had your samples on Thursday, I'd have Friday to prepare slides for microscopic analysis and by Monday morning your cultures should be ready. That's about the only time I could give you for several months. I'm not certain of my colleagues' schedules but we're very busy now. Things may slack off this summer," he said.

Lydia broke into his conversation, "I'll do my best, but I do have a lot of work to do. I guess I'd better get started. Give me your phone number and directions as to where I should come on Thursday," she said.

The technician gave her the information.

"How do I collect the samples, and in what kind of a container?" she asked.

"Purchase a box of one dozen quart canning jars, boil them and the lids for thirty minutes in a pan where they are totally covered with water. Boil tongs in the pot also. Remove the lids and jars. Don't touch the inside of the jars or the lids once you remove them from the water. Place the lids on the jars and lightly seal all. Don't screw the lids down tightly, or the jars may seal and you'll have trouble getting the lids off."

He continued, "Mark the jars as to the place of the collection. Use a permanent marker on the top of the lid.

When collecting the water samples, simply open the sterile jar. Hold the lid in one hand, the jar in the other; dip up a water sample; don't touch anything else with either the lid or the jar. Recap the jar and screw the lid on tight. Place the jar in an upright position, probably in the box the jars came in, or in some kind of padded box so they stay upright and don't bang against each other. If possible, collect at the entry to the impoundment, at the middle and at the outflow. You can even go downstream a mile or two and make another collection."

"What about the soil samples?" Lydia asked. "How do I go about that?"

"You will only use, maybe a half dozen jars for the water, so use the balance of your sterilized jars for the soil. Clean the spade or trowel thoroughly, wash it with soap and water. Then sterilize that in your big pot of water. Air dry and then place your clean shovel and trowel in a large clean plastic bag. These are preliminary, so you can use the same shovel or trowel without further cleaning."

"Collect the sample from the soil's surface and down about six inches. Place what you can into one of the jars and seal that. Again, mark the general location. Since it is around an impoundment of water, you can use the same designation you use for the water jars, such as upper, middle, lower, and below."

"Do you think you understand or do you want me to go over that again?" he asked.

"I think I understand. My mother used to can a little and I think I remember some of her sterilization, so that isn't too foreign to me," Lydia said.

"I know it all sounds a bit complicated, but if you bring contaminated samples, they are of no value. It would be a shame to make the distant drive you mentioned, and then have results that were of no value. If that's all, then I'll look for you on Thursday. Make it as early in the day as you can to give me the most time to work," he said.

She asked for, and received his name and home contact information.

They signed off with, "I'll be looking for you on Thursday," he said.

"I hope to be there. Thank you, you've been most helpful. I've got a lot to accomplish, so I'd better get started" she said.

When she arrived at Carmen's, she made a request. "Can I talk to you a minute?"

Tim played with his trucks on the rings of color on the rug under Carmen's dining table. The varied colors made good roads for his imaginary trips.

The two women went to the bedroom. Carmen went in first, sat on the bed, and turned back to Lydia. Lydia looked back toward Tim and softly closed the door.

"Carmen, I need to make a trip to Fort Collins, but I have to make a few preparations first. Then when I return, I need to go by Colorado Springs for an appointment on Thursday. I can make the preparations this weekend, but I need to be gone most of next week, probably I'd need to start on Monday. I haven't looked at the weather predictions, but if it looks bad, I'd need to start sooner," Lydia said.

Carmen looked stunned. "Do you have to do this during the winter? Can't it wait until later in the year when the weather is better and you're assured of more days with clear roads?"

"I could, but it's important to me that it be done as soon as possible. I really hate to ask you, but do you think you could keep Tim, take him to school each day, and keep him here with you at night? I'll pay you."

" I have a cell phone, sometimes in the mountains the reception isn't good, but I'd call every day and you should be able to reach me some of the time. I have a form filled out, which I keep for his grandparents. It gives permission to take him for medical attention, should an emergency arise. I have their information all written out too, so you could contact them if you thought necessary" Lydia rushed the information.

"Dixie can stay at home, but you and Tim would need to go by everyday, or I can take her to her old master to be boarded for a week."

"No need for boarding Dixie. She and Tim would miss each other too much and she's very good company. Actually, she's better than some human guests I've had. But wow, you give me a scare with all this medical stuff. I've baby sat before, but I've never had to even think about all this. Sure, I'll keep him, but you don't have to pay me," Carmen said.

"But I really need to pay you, I don't want to impose on anyone. I've tried very hard since Scott's gone to be independent," Lydia said.

"I know you have, but friends are here to help friends. You've always been there for me and I want to be here for you," Carmen got up and gave Lydia a hug.

"About all I can say is, *Bon Voyage!*" Carmen said. "Bring what they need and we'll be fine, whichever day you wish. I don't have any big plans for next week, so it will be Tim's and Dixie's vacation away from home. I'll make it seem like fun for him and he won't even miss you. Ha, I know that's not true. You three are joined at the hip, in a good way," Carmen laughed.

"Thank you so much. When I get this all worked out, I'll explain, but now Tim and I had better hit the road and get a few preparations made. I've already missed a day of school, so I'd better be there tomorrow and talk to my principal about taking some personal leave next week," Lydia said.

"Tell him it has to do with Scott's affairs and he won't give you any problems. He's a good guy," Carmen said.

"It is sort of about Scott's affairs but I won't give him a definite reason, unless he asks," Lydia said.

"Lydia, are you going to be doing all this driving by yourself?" Carmen frowned. "Maybe you should take Dixie with you. Tim will be with me."

"So far, no one else is in on this and I'd like to keep it that way. I will be going alone. The less said to the fewer, the better, and Tim will need Dixie worse than I do," Lydia said.

"Will you contact Scott's parents while you're at Fort Collins?" Carmen asked.

"I can't involve Scott's parents. It's too painful," Lydia moaned.

Lydia made a game of preparing the jars with Timmy. After they cooled, she let him set the sterilized jars with the lids into the partitioned box. She took the permanent green marker and labeled each of the jars on the top of the lids. She had chosen a new type of white lid she had never seen before, but she felt would show the markings better and there were fewer parts to handle.

She dug out her trowel and borrowed a soil sampler from her neighbor. She had seen him testing his garden and lawn in the past and was familiar with the object. They had a conversation last spring about how the test should be made and how superior his tool was because it had a place to put one's foot to force the tool into the ground. Lydia realized it would go into the ground more easily, especially if the ground was frozen, and it wouldn't require as large a hole.

She would be able to push the tubular sample into the mouth of the jars more easily than from a shovel blade. She gathered a large screw driver to punch the sample from the sampling pipe should it be frozen or tacky.

She let Timmy scrub the tools in a bucket in the garage with a big brush. Then they took them to the laundry tub and did a second scrub with sink cleanser.

After a thorough rinse, she placed them into the water bath she still had on the burner of her range.

They air-dried the tools on a bed of clean paper towels and then placed them into a large zippered plastic bag she had left from their sleeping bag storage.

"Mom, can I go on your adventure with you?" Tim asked.

"This time, you and Dixie are going on an adventure with Miss Carmen. She'll get you from your class on Monday at the end of the school day and pick up Dixie from home, along with her food. I'll put all of Dixie's stuff by the back door for you. Don't forget to show Carmen where all the dog stuff is. I've got a strong garbage bag you can put it in."

Lydia continued, "She'll take you home with her and you can play on her rug with your trucks again. We'll pack up your little suitcase with several days worth of outfits, we'll put your toys into my big satchel and you can take along your fuzzy blanket if you want. We'll put in a couple of pair of PJs."

" Is there anything else you want to take? If you need more, I'll give Carmen a key and you can come home to get extras."

"She even has some surprises for you. She will give you one each day and when I get home, you can show me what you got," Lydia said.

"Miss Carmen has a lot of things planned for you. I'm leaving her some money for your favorite pizza. I expect you'll go out to eat a couple of times. I'll hurry and only be gone a few days. I promise I'll call every day and I should be home by Thursday evening. If it snows a whole lot, I might need to stay at a motel, but I'll call. We can work that out when the time comes."

Lydia didn't pack her own bags until Timmy was

asleep. She didn't want to worry him. She put in heavy, outdoor wear for herself, her hooded parka, heavy clothes, silk long Johns, boots and snowshoes. She also included a backpack she could fit the jars into for the samples.

As the very last item, she placed Scott's pistol and a box of shells into the outer pocket of her backpack. She put all her items in the trunk of the car.

At school on Monday, she took Timmy to his class and hugged him good by. He took his new Show and Tell truck and moved into his class room. She handed his teacher a note giving permission for him to go with Miss Carmen after school. The office already had the same information.

After she had ushered him into his classroom, she gave Carmen all of Timmy's items from the trunk of her car. She had added some wrapped packages for him to open each day. She included several extra, in case they ran out of things to do. She had put in his favorite games and tucked in some snacks. Dixie had her own pack by the door for when they picked her up after school.

"Wow, is he staying for a month?" Carmen said. "There is enough here to go on Safari."

"I know, this is the first time I've left him since Scott has been gone and I guess I overdid it a bit." Lydia sniffled. "Sorry, it's letting him grow up a little and I am having a hard time with that. I want him with me always and I know that isn't going to happen. He's already growing up too fast."

"It's okay, be on your way and we'll be fine. It's not like I don't take care of twenty-three kids every day. Surely we can find something to do," Carmen joked.

Dressed in jeans and her outdoor wear, Lydia hit the road to Fort Collins. She hadn't been back for a time and she looked forward to seeing some of their old stomping grounds, but the collection process concerned her.

Will someone try to stop me? I won't try to avoid

seeing other people, but I want to blend in. There may be some there who know me, but I'm not going to deliberately look anyone up. From being around the reservoir, I know what the students wear.

I feel like a criminal, but I have to protect others and the animals.

Her drive to Fort Collins was uneventful. The sun shone and it was hard to believe that it was January. Lydia always liked to drive and she was able to get on US-285 after about sixty miles. By the time she reached US-24, she stopped for a break and to fill her gas tank. She replenished her thermos with coffee and grabbed a burger before she hit the road. She had apples, bananas, and oranges in the seat beside her, along with a bag of trail mix and energy bars. Six bottles of water were in a cooler in the trunk, along with more fruit. The cooler wasn't to keep things cool, but to keep some items from freezing. She would replace those items with her sample jars of water, once she collected those.

She reached Fort Collins by dusk and found an inside hallway motel close to the ramp on Mulberry Street. Her intention was to arise early in the morning, drive to the outlaying research campus, and take her hike around the reservoir for the samples.

Lydia picked up a take-out Chinese meal and then settled into her motel. She called Timmy and Carmen as soon as she was inside safe for the night.

Carmen answered on the second ring. "Hi, this is the residence of a school teacher and her little friend for the next few days."

"It's me, I'm here and in the motel, all safe and sound with a couple of Chinese boxes of take-out cashew chicken

and a few other items. Everything went well. How are you all doing?" she asked.

"We're great. We got a lot of attention at the Pizza Village. Some said he was too short to be my new man, but I told them, just never you mind, we're having a blast. Here I'll let you talk to my boy friend?" Carmen joked.

"Hi, Mom. Where are you?" Timmy asked.

"I'm all checked into a motel here at Fort Collins. You know that's the town where Daddy and I used to go to college. I'm in a big hurry, so I won't be able to visit Daddy's parents while I'm here." She changed the subject, "I just got a fortune cookie, want me to open it for you?"

"Sure, I like those," he said.

"I know you do. I should have gotten two so I could bring one home to you. I'm cracking it, here goes, here's the fortune, and it says: You are a good boy and Mom loves you!" she said.

"It does not, you are trying to fool me. What does it say?" he asked.

"It says, You are going to meet a beautiful person. You already know Carmen, so let's make it a beautiful woman. You can tell her when you get off that she's a beautiful woman. Ladies like to hear that from their men friends."

"Aw, Mom," he said.

"Did you have fun today at school?" Lydia asked.

"We had finger paint and I got it all over me. Miss Carmen had to put me in the tub when we got home. I couldn't go to the Pizza Village with all that stuff dried on my arms. We got it off and had fun when we went for our pizza. Now, we're playing with my trucks on the roads on her rug. Her table makes a good tent. We put some blankets over the chairs. Dixie and I may sleep here tonight. It feels kind of like our tent at our cabin in the mountains," Tim said.

Lydia yawned. "Well, Tim, I seem to be sleepy, guess

it's about our bedtime. You give Miss Carmen a hug for me and tell her thanks. Have a good night and I'll talk to you again tomorrow. I'm going to hike around some trails tomorrow, so my phone may not work for a little bit, but if it doesn't, I'll call from a motel tomorrow evening. I love you, Buddy. Have pleasant dreams and be good for Miss Carmen," Lydia said. A tear trickled down her cheek.

"Night, Mom. Wish you were here," Tim said. "Here, Miss Carmen, do you want to tell Mommy good night?"

"We're fine, don't worry and we'll hear from you tomorrow. Anything you need to tell me?" Carmen asked.

Lydia say, "No, just take care of my little guy and thanks again. Bye, for now."

"Okay, we'll be thinking of you. We'll offer a prayer for you tonight when we hop into bed. Love you, Bye," Carmen hung up.

Lydia replaced the phone and buried her face in the crisp white pillow.

She didn't sleep well. The noises were different than those at home and she never slept well the first night in different places. Several times during the night, she prayed for Timmy and Carmen.

Please Lord, take care of them.

Am I doing the right thing? Please don't let this hurt anyone or the University. Help me find anything that is wrong, but if it's okay, let me find that too.

Thank you, Lord, for all the blessings you've given me, especially Tim now, the time I had with Scott too. You blessed us, even though it wasn't for a long time together.

More tears stained her pillow that night. She felt especially lonely, but arose in the morning with new resolve to get the job done and get on home.

She listened to the early news. The weatherman predicted a front coming in that would dump several inches of snow in the mountains.

Even if it does snow today, I've got to get out on the trail and get the job done, so I can get started back.

She hurried to put her gear in order. She dressed in layers of clothing with jeans on the outside.

She had packed her backpack at home with the soil sampling tools. It was ready to go. She checked the jars. She had seven in the pack ready to go. All were intact and well padded with towels from home and a space blanket folded several times to a small size. She checked Scott's pistol again and filled the magazine. She left the chamber open, replaced it in the backpack and hung her hatchet on the outside loop.

She checked out of her room, drove to the parking lot at the remote University campus, and parked at the head of the reservoir in a visitor's parking lot. She pulled on her gear. Her snow shoes were tied to the outside of her pack. She slipped in extra energy bars and trail mix. Two bottles of water joined the pack next to her body and she was ready to hit the trail. She locked her car and zipped her cell phone into the pocket of her parka.

She walked up on the dam that prevented ground water from entering the reservoir at the upper end. Lydia looked around, then squatted to dip the first jar into the water. She was nervous and clicked it on a rock. A hole broke. She retrieved another jar and was very careful this time to fill the jar three fourths full. She screwed on the lid without touching any of the debris from the water, or on the bank. She carefully wrapped a towel around the jar and inserted it back into her pack. She scooped soil from the dam, prepared the second jar and inserted that next to the first in her pack.

Guess I should have started at the other end and then I wouldn't have to carry the extra weight there and back. I've already learned two lessons. Don't break your sample jar and don't carry your samples any further than necessary.

Oh, well, gotta start somewhere. Here I go, I'm trekking out and then I'll come back. I'd better get a move on if I'm going to make the whole trail and get my samples in one day.

She went back to the trunk of her car and placed the first samples in the cooler. She deposited the broken jar in a refuse bag and threw the jar lid back into her trunk.

Now to get started again.

Lydia started over. *I have a good load. Carrying the extra weight of the samples would have been a poor idea.*

She walked steadily. *This isn't a time to waste effort or look at the forests and animals, which are scarce this time of year.*

A few magpies scolded her. One flew along and kept her company with his conversation.

During her lunch break, she placed a bit of her energy bar on a stump and he flew down to join her meal.

By noon, she reached the farthest reaches of her hike. She took her water sample from the outflowing stream of water two miles down the little valley. She removed her soil sampler and managed to get a good core sampling of the soil. She placed both samples, and the tool, wrapped in several paper towels, back into their assigned places and started the return trip.

She took another set of soil and water samples at the point of overflow from the reservoir.

About three miles into her return hike, she met a man on the trail. A thrill of fear sped down her spine and speeded her heart rate.

The man spoke and she returned his words with a nod. She hurried on up the trail. Around a bend, she checked Scott's pistol and chambered a shell. She checked to be sure

the safety was on and replaced the handgun in the outer

pocket of her pack.

I never felt this way when Scott was along on our hikes. Our hikes were so much more fun. I hate being afraid of people, when they are out enjoying God's world. Please help me lose this fear, but. . . keep me safe. Lord, I am afraid.

She stopped in about thirty minutes to take the midway samples. The pack was growing heavier by the mile.

As soon as she got back on the trail, she heard branches and twigs snapping behind her.

She went behind a tree and slipped the hatchet head into her hand. The handle aligned with her arm. None of the hatchet showed beyond her bulky glove and parka.

She hurried her steps. The sounds came closer.

I'm so glad I collected those first samples when I first got out. By the time I get back to my car, I'm going to be running, if that sound doesn't back off.

He's probably hurrying to be in before it gets dark too. I should slow down, but. . . I can't.

I see the trees at the parking lot. Thank you, Lord. I think I'm going to make it.

She hurried her foot steps and reached into her pocket for her keys. She put her finger on the red alert button, in case the follower got too close. As far as she knew, there was no one else around to come to her assistance, but it made her feel a little safer.

She scrambled into her car, punched the lock on her door, nestled the hatchet into her console, placed her backpack of samples gently in the passenger floor, inserted her key, and sprinted out of the parking lot.

I'll put my samples away when I get some distance from this place and back into civilization.

I'm driving too fast to get away from this isolated area.

Finally, I see other vehicles.

At the first junction I saw a convenience store when I went in. I'll pull next to the building, under the lights which just came on. I'll look around, pick up my pack and exit the car. Get into the restroom, lock the door and organize myself.

She breathed a sigh, sat on the stool and cried.

When she regained some control, she removed the pistol from her pack, took out the shells and placed them back into the box. She packed the pistol behind the jars. Lydia washed her face and went out to the counter to purchase a soft drink. She didn't want it, but felt badly using their facilities without some compensation.

She walked to the front of the store, looked in all directions and returned to her car.

She looked around. No one was watching or parked near her car. She carefully took the jars from her pack and stowed them in the cooler. She closed the trunk lid and put her pack in the front seat again.

It took only a few minutes to return to her motel.

She collapsed on the bed as soon as she locked the door to her motel room.

I didn't have much lunch. I'm famished. As soon as I get over the jitters, I'll order-in. I don't care what, I just want to stay in and be quiet.

After a few minutes, she removed her small Bible from her backpack and looked at some of the verses Scott had read to her so often. She paraphrased some of Scott's favorites. *My strength cometh from God. I will lift up mine eyes to the hills from whence cometh my strength.* She looked for the proper references. She didn't find all his favorites but enough to calm her fear.

After an hour, she picked up the menu from the bedside table. She punched in the numbers and ordered

breakfast for dinner. Belgian waffles with berries, an egg and two sausage links.

What a good hot meal.

After she had eaten, she called Tim from her cell phone. They didn't talk long.

She spoke to Carmen, "Mission Accomplished! I'm on the road to Colorado Springs in the morning. I'll keep you posted. I didn't sleep well last night, so I'm hitting the sack early and I'll probably get up early, so I had better sign off."

Tim had gone back to his newest surprise.

Carmen softly spoke before she could hang up. "Look at the weather news. That storm seems about ready to roll in. Be careful in the morning. Your roads will be on the east side of the mountains which will help. Be really careful when you start back west after the delivery. Keep in touch, we love you."

"I am being very careful. I'll tell you all about it when I get home. Thanks again. I love you both too. Bye."

Lydia snapped her phone closed and lay it carefully on the bedside table.

She stood under the spray of a hot shower for a very long time. She began to relax. The mirror was steamed when she put on her PJs, her robe, and went into her room. She had already turned down the covers, so she collapsed and pulled up the blanket and comforter.

Lydia rose long enough to pack her belongings and was ready to hit the road to the lab in Colorado Springs early the next morning.

She lay back down in her still warm bed. *My mind isn't turned off. Wish I hadn't been so afraid on the trail today. Why can't a woman go out alone? They shouldn't have to be scared out of their wits every time some man comes along. I think I'll sign up for that self-defense class at the Y when I get back to Gunnison. I had the gun, but it would have taken me a little to get it out of the pack. I might not have had that much time.*

Good I had the hatchet, but there is no way I could over-power a person of that size.

She began to drift. *Maybe I'll get some pepper spray too. I'll enroll Tim in a karate class, so he won't worry about me taking self-defense classes. It will be good exercise for both of us.*

She had fearful dreams. She sometimes ran from something, but she didn't know who, or what.

Lydia slept hard, but awakened early. Lazy snow flakes had started, but there was no build-up on the roads. Lydia made good time to Colorado Springs. The one hundred and thirty or so miles were just a good warm-up for the day.

If I can find the lab and this guy, I can be on my way a day early and surprise Tim when I pick him up at school. That's pushing it a bit, if it takes long at the lab, but I might make it.

She pulled into Colorado Springs in time for lunch. She called the lab technician from her cell phone and arranged for a meeting time.

She used her GPS to locate the address he gave for the lab. The receptionist admitted her to a high security reception area and a man dressed totally in white came out to meet her.

She extended her hand, "Hello, I'm Lydia Thayer. I have the samples in this cooler. I put them in there yesterday to keep them from freezing last night. I looked this morning and they seem to be in good shape. Where do you want me to put them?" she asked.

"Let me carry that for you. Come right this way," he said. "If you want to wait around a couple of hours, I might be able to get a few tests run this afternoon."

Lydia looked crestfallen.

"I had hoped to get on the road right after I gave you the samples. Is it worth my time to hang around, or would it be better to hear the total results when you finish? I'm a widow,

my little boy is with a friend. This is the first time I've left him
since my husband died. I'm sorry, I'm running on and you're
not interested in all my situations," she apologized.

"You won't need to remain, I thought perhaps you were
very eager to hear, but that's okay. I'll get the results out next
week. Thank you for being so prompt. The receptionist will get
your credit card number and take care of the billing. She has an
estimate of probable costs. If there's any problem, she'll let
me know. I'll call with the first results, then an itemized
account will follow," he said. If further tests are needed, we'll
need to go gather our own samples, but we won't proceed
further until you give us the go ahead. At that time, we would
have a further estimate as to cost."

"Thank you very much and thanks for being so quick
to take care of this for me. I'm praying for the results hoped
for. I will hit the road and thanks again," Lydia said.

"Watch out for that snow storm blowing in. Your
mountain drive to Gunnison may be a whopper today. You'd
better find a motel early and hole up until this blows over."

"I'll certainly take that into consideration. Thanks again
and I'll be hearing from you," Lydia scooted out the door and
into her still warm car. Her deflated backpack lay on the seat
next to her.

Now the jars are in someone else's hands. I can only
pray for negative results for Scott, and the University.

By two in the afternoon, the wind blew the snow so
hard, Lydia had trouble seeing the edges of the road. Few other
travelers were on the road. She passed Penrose, then by-passed
Portland and Florence which had business routes. She saw no
motels there. She pressed on and realized she'd never get over
the next couple of passes with the snow blowing as it was.

She finally pulled into Salida.

I can not see. Even though I am more than halfway

home to Tim, I can go no further. It would be foolish to end up off one of these cliffs. I might not be found until spring, if then. What would our son do? I must stop, even if I have to sit up in a truck stop overnight. I'll park, check my GPS and see if they have motels listed.

Several motels were listed on Highway 50. Lydia choose the closest and pulled under the canopy to see if they had accommodations.

The canopy cut the driving snow. She could see to exit her car and reach the slick sidewalk without falling down. She walked gingerly into the foyer and shook her coat before entering the lobby.

The sleepy clerk looked up. "Not many out tonight, they don't want to brave this gale. Need a room?" he asked.

"Yeah, I have to give up. I can't see to drive any further and I've yet to get over the last passes. They always seem to be the worst part of a mountain drive. I'll need a room for one. I would prefer it near the office, or on the side protected from the snow," Lydia said.

"Got just what you want. You can have the inside room here to my left, it is non-smoking. I try to hold on to it for ladies when they come in by themselves. You can come and go through the lobby and park your car in the first sections to the left of the entry. There may already be a lot of snow in the parking spots, so move to any you find that are better on this side. I'm sorry your car will be in a lot of snow tonight, but if I put you on the other side out of the snow, you're a long ways from the lobby. There aren't many here now so you'd be over there by yourself. I don't expect many more in tonight, unless we'd get a bus or a group who can't travel in this snow. That's not likely," he added.

"What's the price of the room on your left?" Lydia

asked. *It doesn't matter, I've got to take it, no matter what price he gives.*

"That would be sixty-five for one person occupancy. It is ski season and we normally get more, but with this blizzard, no skiers are going up tomorrow or maybe even the next day. I doubt you'll be able to go on over this road tomorrow unless this wind dies down and the plows really get moving. You want one day or two? It's a little cheaper for multiple days," he commented.

"I'll just take one for now. I sure hope I can get out tomorrow. I don't have too far to go, I could wait a little bit later tomorrow and hope they plow out these roads," Lydia said.

"Check out time is eleven AM, if you stay past that, we'll have to charge you for another day," the clerk said.

"That's fine. I'll know by mid-morning if there is a chance for me to move on," Lydia reached for a registration form on his desk.

"I'll need a credit card or cash up front. If you use the phone, it will go through our switch board. If you don't have a calling card, it won't go," he said.

"I have my cell. I'll use it," she said.

"If you get a signal. Some do and some don't. You'll have to try it and see. We are up high, but sometimes they won't go, depends on your service provider," the student replied.

"It seems to be that, no matter where we go, especially in the mountains." She turned the card toward the clerk. "There, is that all the information you need?"

"May I have your credit card and some identification?" he asked.

Lydia drew out her driver's license and her credit card. He ran the card through his machine and handed back her two cards.

"We have a continental breakfast from six through ten

Feel free to partake whenever you wish. There is an ice machine in our breakfast room to the right. There are some vending machines in there, or the restaurant connected at the end of the units is open. It should be open all night. They will come here, if you wish to order from their menu, which is in your room. Are you going to need help in with your luggage?" he asked.

"No, I'm good. I am traveling light tonight," she replied.

"Want a wake-up call or anything else tonight?" he asked. "I'm going off-duty in about an hour. The next clerk will be in the rooms behind this desk. If you have a need, ring the bell and he should hear. You may have to ring it more than once, but he's back there and he's supposed to be on duty. Sometimes he drifts off to sleep or gets caught up in his movies. Have a good night," he saluted Lydia and turned back to his computer screen.

Lydia flipped the hood up on her parka and went back out into the storm to park her car and retrieve her overnight case.

She came back into the foyer and flipped open her cell phone to check for a signal. If it was better here, she might have to come back from her room and make a call to Tim and Carmen from nearer the outside doors. The signal was good, so she hoped the same would apply in her room.

When Lydia tried the key card, the door opened easily. She let herself into the room, then turned to latch the door and the chain. She flipped her phone open again and punched in Carmen's home number.

They answered on the second ring.

"Where are you?" Carmen asked quietly.

"I had to stop at Salido. I got as far as I could, but there was no visibility, so I had to pull in. I should be able to make it easily by tomorrow afternoon. They aren't giving a lot of encouragement from this end, but if I have to wait until after noon, surely they will have it passable by then," she said. "I'm at th Salido Inn. It's right on the highway, so I'll be near if the plows run."

"Don't try it, if the visibility is low and the roads haven't been cleared. We're doing great. I'm having more fun than I've had for a long while. Tim is one of the best dates I've ever had. He's a jewel and I could get used to having him and Dixie around. Do you want to talk to him. He's already in bed, but he's waited for your call since we got in from school. He was a little worried about you, but I encouraged him to go to bed and play with his small video game while he waited to go to sleep. I hear him now, he heard the phone ring. I'd better take the cordless to him or he'll be up again. Hang on for a moment," Carmen said.

"Hello, Mom?" Tim asked.

"Hi, Buddy. Carmen says you are doing great. I'm very proud of you acting such a big man for her and Mom," Lydia said.

"Why didn't you call sooner?" he asked.

"I was in a lot of snow and thought I'd better find me a motel before it got any worse. I didn't get away from Colorado Springs until after lunch and it took me longer than I thought it would. I thought maybe I'd get home tonight, but the snow is really coming down, so I stopped off here in Solida. I've got a nice room but it sure would be fun if you were here with me. We'll have to come back and go skiing one of these days," Lydia said. "The ski slopes here look really good. We'd try the little runs first. How about that?" she asked.

"Sounds like fun. Did you get your hike?" he asked.

"I sure did. I went back where Daddy and I used to hike and work, then I came and talked to a man. You know the jars we fixed? He's got them now. He's going to look at the dirt and water I collected through a microscope," she explained.

"Will he keep our jars?" Tim asked.

"Yes, I don't think I'll drive back for them, it's too far. We can buy some more at the store. Do you want to can some of the apples from our tree this summer?" Lydia asked.

"That would be fun. Would we put them in jars like those we had?" he asked.

"I think we'd get the smaller ones for our apples. We don't have too many, unless we bought some more. I think the smaller jars would be fine. I still have some of the caps. I accidentally broke one on a rock, so I saved that lid. I'm bringing it back with me. We can make some apple jelly. Your Grandma Brown makes apple jelly. We'll have her show us how when she comes, how about that?" Lydia asked.

"That would be fun, Mom. When are you coming home?" he asked.

"If the snow is cleared and it quits, I think I can make it by the time you're ready for bed tomorrow, maybe even sooner, but if they don't get out the snow plows, I may be stranded here another day. I've got a nice motel room and I can stay on more, if I need to. You know I want to get home, so we both need to be patient," Lydia said. "You go on to school tomorrow and we'll see if I can get in by bedtime," she said.

"You know, I've about decided you and I are going to the Y for some lessons. I think it's about time you signed up for Karate lessons. I'll take some lessons too and we'll have a lot of fun. Eat well, get your muscles to growing well and we'll see how we do in some classes. Would you like that?" she asked.

"I sure would, that will be fun. My friend at school takes karate lessons, maybe I'll be in his class," Tim said.

"We'll do it when I get home. Now, sleep tight. I love you, Buddy," Lydia said.

"Me, too, Mom. You sleep tight too."

Lydia heard Tim yawn into the phone.

"Sounds like you're about there already?"

"I am. You called, now I can go to sleep. Night, Mom," he said.

Carmen took the phone, "Hang on a minute, Lydia." She covered Tim, went out the bedroom door, and gently closed it.

"We're fine, take your time and we'll see you when you get here," Carmen said quietly. "The main thing is for you to be safe, don't take any chances. Better a day late than to have a problem along the road. Take care and we're still praying for you. Love you, Lydia," Carmen said.

"Okay, MOTHER, I'll be good. I will be careful and I'll see you both when I get there. I can hardly wait. I have a load off my mind already when I delivered all those samples and nothing bad happened along the way. I'll tell you all about it when I get home. Thank you, so much. Good night, Carmen," Lydia said.

The snow plows hadn't gotten to the mountain road when Lydia arose in the morning, but by the time she walked to the restaurant for lunch, they drove into the lot for their lunch. She walked over to the men and asked about the road toward Gunnison.

"Over the top, it is one-way, but well-cleared in the one lane. If you drive slowly, honk at curves, you can make it. Don't get out of the one lane. We will be back that way later today," one man said.

" If you meet someone, one of you is going to have to back about a quarter of a mile, so better hope any meetings are close to one of the turn-arounds," the man said. "You can probably make the thirty miles in about an hour and a half. Then after you get about half-way, the road is opened into Gunnison. Still don't get out of the cleared areas. We left the sides about six-feet tall, some places more. We filled in some holes, so you'd never know if you were driving into a flat spot or off the side of the cliff," he cautioned.

"That sounds excellent, I think I'll grab a sandwich to take along and hit the road. I need to get back to my son. Thank you for your good work. I appreciate it and I'm sure there are a lot of other folks in the same boat. Have a good day," Lydia called as she turned to go toward the restaurant counter.

She arrived in Gunnison by the time Tim and Carmen were ready to go home from school.

Lydia put Tim into her car and drove behind Carmen to her house.

Dixie greeted all of them enthusiastically. She leaned into Lydia's knee.

After initial clinging, Tim showed her the roads on Carmen's rug he used for his cars and started to play apart from the two women.

Lydia filled Carmen in on all that had happened, including her scare on the trail, the collection of the samples, and her experience with the lab technician.

"I should have an answer by next week. He was starting on it yesterday afternoon and said if I'd hang around, he would have some answers in a couple of hours. I told him I'd like to get home, to give me the final results all at one time. He's going to call and then send a legal written report."

A tear escaped down Lydia's cheek, "Oh, Carmen, pray everything is negative and there was nothing out there that made Scott sick. I can't stand the thought of the University having any involvement or any problems now that would have to be cleaned up. No one would have done anything deliberately and this kind of thing would open a can of worms that would be hard to handle. I'd have trouble handling it. His illness is enough on my mind, without this kind of thing to haunt me."

She continued, " I don't like that law firm attempting to get rich on blood money. They could cost the University millions and then everyone could still be proven innocent, but the money for many programs would be gone. Some students would be adversely affected and some might even be injured, health wise. Pray!" Lydia gritted her teeth.

"I did this for Scott, for Tim, for all the students that have been in the forestry department at the University, and for God's Creation. Whatever the outcome, I will know I did what I should."

"If I get a negative report, I am going to send that firm a copy and a letter telling them to quit their litigation or I will turn the report over to the news media. They wouldn't want bad publicity," Lydia said. "I'll send a copy to the University too. They need to know and cut this thing off before it gets blown up and causes everyone problems."

Carmen patted her arm. "You are riled. Nothing like a woman angered, or is that scorned? Anyway, whatever. Go get 'em Lydia," Carmen raised her fist.

"Well, I'm kind of tired. I better get the kids and hit the road. I expect you'll be glad for the weekend so you can rest from your BIG date you've had most of this week. I can't repay you. Thank you so much, Carmen. You are a very good friend and we don't know what we'd do without you," she hugged Carmen. "Thank you, thank you, Lady. Anytime you want something, just ask. If it is within our power, Tim, Dixie, and I will give it to you."

"No more thanks needed. You both take care and I'll see you at school next week." Carmen patted Lydia on the back.

"Say, you should come visit us at our cabin in the mountain this summer. That would give you a rest and you could see where we live part of the year," Lydia said.

"I'd like that. I like to hike and be in the great outdoors. I just may take you up on that," Carmen said. "We'll make plans closer to summer when we see what everyone is going to do."

"Tim, time to hit the road for home. Do you have all your belongings collected?" The four made a search for any left-over objects. Lydia zipped the suitcase.

On Thursday afternoon, Lydia received a call during her lunch hour. She went to the empty gymnasium to receive the lab reports. She gripped her phone tightly and closed the fist of her other hand. Nervous tension rippled through her body.

The technician started his report. "We found absolutely nothing unusual in your samples for forest and lake areas. We have carefully labeled the results and they will be arriving by certified letter. The results have been notarized, so this is a legal document, as you requested. One of our personnel can also give an affidavit, if needed for the court system. If some wish to refute our tests, we can return and take our own samples, even under their watchful eye, and with the same areas, the results should be the same."

"A copy of your bill will be included. It is nominal, as we needed to go no further with the testing. If you have more need of anything from our lab, please contact us. Thank you for your trust in our company. Do you have any questions?" he asked.

"Praise the Lord!" Lydia was overcome with emotion for a moment, "I thank you, you found just the answers I hoped for. This should take away any liability the University has and also should stop the law firm trying to capitalize on something that never happened. I can't thank you enough. You have taken a huge burden off me, by verifying that my husband did not die of any pollutant while doing research at that site. I can't tell you how much I appreciate your promptness too. I never expected to have results within a week," she exclaimed.

"That was unusual. You caught us exactly at the right time for a quick answer. Had you contacted us, even a day or so later, we would have had several months delay before we could have run your tests and gotten back your results."

"Ma'am, I have to say that all this seemed Providential. I am a scientist, but I am also a Christian. I do believe the Lord moves in mysterious ways and He's done it again. Thank you, Ma'am for another piece of evidence in my exploration of God's control of His Creation and all that entails. I can't always say this to our clients, but this time I have a prompting that He had a hand in this and that you should be given that message."

"You are so right. He does control His Creation and He has given me repeated evidence that He's with us and He loves us. He just keeps providing. Thank you again," Lydia said.

"I need to get back to work. God bless you, Mrs. Thayer. Hope you continue in good health and happiness with your son," the technician said. He hung up the phone.

Lydia flipped her phone closed and danced a circle on the gymnasium floor. "Thank you, Lord, Thank you."

She wrote her letters and sent the documents. She included a statement to the law firm which proved her point as to the collection sites. The University received a copy of the same materials.

You may think that I got the samples at an incorrect place. However, I was engaged to Scott and spent many hours that summer working with him on this particular site. As you stated in your own words, we planted trees the summer of 1998, on the Valley Site on the Forest Ridge property.

Many of Scott's friends also worked on that site that

summer, and I know they are still alive and well. Several came to be with us at Scott's death. I have contacted each one of them and they assure me they have not had, and are not now having any health issues.

I was very familiar with where my fiancee worked and these friends worked, and what they did because I was there also.

I am still healthy and have had a blood test to see if my body contains any contaminants. The medical profession found none. Your theory of pollutants at the University site is now thoroughly disproved, by the soil and water samples, and my healthy report.

The foremost testing laboratory in this area found negative results for anything out of the ordinary for healthy forest floors, water sheds, and reservoir water. The forwarded results should lay your law firm's cases on campus pollution to rest.

It is my hope I hear nothing further from you, but should you persist, I am prepared to fight your prosecution of the University and release my information and your actions to the media.

Lydia signed her name, folded the letter and sealed the envelope.

There, that's one unpleasant task finished.

Lydia breathed a sigh of relief.

Now I can move on and forget this saga. I did it for Scott and everyone else who will be involved with that parcel of land.

Thank you, Lord for another wonderful provision for my family.

The Fishing Expedition

That summer, Pastor Jeff arrived a day early to prepare for the fishing expedition. He had made arrangements for Tim and Lydia's fishing license.

Archie planned to go along, but Vera had elected to stay and "mind the store."

Lydia and Tim arrived at the cabin, they were so exhausted, they planned to go to bed soon after their arrival. Tim jumped out of the car and ran into the yard with Dixie. Lydia unloaded only the bags necessary for bedtime, their groceries, and locked the car on the balance.

I'll let this wait until morning. I'm totally zonked.

Tim and Dixie made their circuit around the yard and walked on the stone wall. Tim was becoming more and more coordinated as he grew each year.

Lydia turned back to her task. She found a note taped to their door.

Archie and I are ready. We have the food, the rods and reels, and permits. We'll see you early in the morning.

Night, Jeff

Lydia was too tired to sleep. During the night, she heard Tim's voice.

I need to check on him. The cabin may have brought back his nightmares.

She found her son twisted in his sheets and turning. Dixie stood by the bed.

Lydia lay her hand on her son's shoulder, "Tim, are you okay?"

He quieted, she placed her palm on his forehead to check for a fever. He remained silent.

"It's okay, Dixie. I think he's just excited and very tired." She rubbed Tim's back until he settled into a peaceful sleep, then slipped from his room. Dixie stayed on guard. She lay beside Tim's bed with her nose turned toward him.

A half hour later, Dixie snored too.

Lydia gave up and put on a pot of decaf coffee. She got her easel and water colors from the closet. She sketched out a trout stream and the background. She yawned, *I'll finish this after today and I see how we do. I'm sleepy.*

She sat down in Scott's old recliner and turned her face into his pillow. *I imagine I can still smell his scent.*

She soon dreamed, dreams filled with Scott and their times in this cabin.

At five-fifteen, Tim and Dixie awakened her. Scott's pillow was clutched in her arms when she awoke.

"You gotta get ready, Mom. They said they'd be here at five-thirty."

"Wow, I guess I went back to sleep. I'll get a cup of coffee. I'll be ready before you can count to one-hundred." She played their old game.

Tim started, "One, two, three. Mom, you're not moving."

Lydia put Scott's pillow back in the chair. She padded to the kitchen and filled her cup.

"It's too hot, I'll dress and then drink it. If they come, give them some coffee and keep them occupied. Okay, Tim?" she asked.

"Okay, Mom. Four, five, six–

She hurried into her bedroom and shut the door. She was back out by the count of seventy-five. She had only slipped on her outerwear of jeans, and a tee shirt, with a sweatshirt on top. She had worn her underwear and socks to bed under a nightshirt.

She hit the bathroom and brushed her short hair. She smirked at herself in the mirror. *So much for ladies being clean on fishing trips.*

She raced back into the main room.

"Eighty-six. Okay, you made it before one hundred, a

new record. Way to go, Mom!" Tim crowed.

"Oh, you," she ruffled his short-cropped curls.

They heard a thump on the deck as the fishing crew arrived.

Tim stuck his head out the door. "Mom says to come get a cup of coffee."

"We've had one, but that was so long ago, think I'll have another," Archie said.

Lydia popped a couple of breakfast sandwiches in the microwave for her and Tim. "Anyone want one of these, we've got a bunch?"

Both men shook their head on a "no."

Tim gobbled down his sandwich. Lydia munched hers.

"We're ready. I got out the best flies last night. Tim and I have our fly rods. I hope the line hasn't rotted. We haven't used them for awhile," Lydia said.

Archie went to the deck to check the rods she had propped against the cabin.

"It's nylon line. It should be okay." He striped out a few feet and tested it between his hands. "The outside loops would be the most exposed and these feel fine. Even though trout are good fighters, they aren't usually real large. You're all set. No tangles and everything smooth as silk. Scott took good care of his equipment."

"Yes, he did and I've probably neglected it. I should have checked those last fall," Lydia said.

Jeff noted she looked a bit downtrodden this morning.

"Everything is fine, we're just in it for some good outdoor time. We've got that roast for dinner if we don't catch anything. Ready, Tim?" Pastor Jeff asked.

"Let's go," Tim hollered.

Archie looked at the group. "Head 'em up, and move 'em out!" he hollered. He led the way.

The rest trouped along three abreast, until the trail

narrowed. Then Tim followed Archie, Lydia next, and Jeff behind to pick up any stragglers. Dixie set her own pace and broke her own trail.

After a half hour, Archie halted. "We're here. Spread out along this stream and have at it. Tim, you stay in sight of the grown-ups. We don't want to have to fish you out."

Lydia and Tim slipped on waders she had slung over her shoulder. The men did the same.

She stuck her hand into the water, "Brr, it is cold. Tim be sure to stay in water no deeper than the mark on the waders. There are holes in the bottom here. Check with your rod or a foot before you walk into a deeper spot," she directed.

Jeff listened to her advice. He hadn't fly fished and was inexperienced. He'd seen a movie once on fishing with flies.

Guess I should have rented a video and learned some things before I got here.

He watched Archie, Lydia and Tim as they played out line and whipped their rods until the line formed an arc over each one. He tried to imitate them and wrapped his line around himself.

Tim looked his way and laughed. "Do you know how to fly fish?"

"Apparently not. I've cast, but never with a fly rod," Jeff said.

Tim reeled in his line. "Watch me, I'll show you how."

Jeff watched closely and tried again, with only slightly better results. Tim tried to untangle him.

"You'll have to cut off a piece of your line and Mom can hook the fly back on at a new place," the boy said.

Jeff felt very foolish, but stepped to Lydia. "Can you show us how to attach this fly to my line?"

"I can do better than that. I'll put it on and then guide your arm so you can feel the action," Lydia said. She quickly tied on his fly and stepped behind him. She gripped his forearm, reached around and tried to catch the line. "Maybe you'd better stand behind me, my arms aren't long enough to help you like we used to help Tim," she said.

Jeff positioned himself behind her.

"Grip the rod over my hand, then reach over to my other hand and the line," she directed.

Jeff was so aware of her, his mind did not function.

"Relax your arms and let me lift them with mine. You'll catch on," she said.

Get a grip man, Jeff scolded himself.

After ten or so lifts, he began to catch on. She let go with her left hand. Thirty or forty feet of line floated out over the water. It landed lightly in a riffle.

"Now you try it," she rewound and handed him her rod.

He was awkward but did manage to play out the line and actually land it a distance out into the water.

"Now, reel it in with slight jerks. Lift the tip of the rod a bit, then wind the reel. That's it. I think you've got it now. Try it with your rod," she said.

"Better step back, I'm not as good as you all. I may hook anyone in sight or the fly may end up behind me," Jeff said.

Lydia walked away and watched as Jeff played out his line and landed it about thirty yards in front of himself. He turned with a triumphant grin.

He's handsome. Lydia turned away quickly.

She spoke with her face toward the ground as she retrieved her rod.

"I'll move away so you have plenty of room to practice. Yell at one of us if you have a problem."

Tim caught the first trout, Archie the second, Lydia the third. All went round again.

Finally Jeff caught one, then himself.

Archie arrived with his pliers. "I'll have to cut off the

shank and shove it through. I can see it just under the skin. It's a small hook, so it shouldn't hurt too much. You ready?" he asked.

"Wait." Lydia retrieved the first aid kit and poured Iodine on Jeff's forearm at the site.

Jeff braced his arm on his thigh. "Ready as I'll ever be. Have at it."

Archie cut off the tiny shank next to Jeff's skin. He shoved the point and barb through and grabbed the point with his pliers, then extracted the hook expertly.

Jeff was surprised. "The point didn't feel as bad as I thought it would when it came through the skin. When it went in, I hardly felt it, it happened so quickly."

Lydia poured on more Iodine.

Jeff drew in a quick breath. "Now, that I felt!"

She dried his arm with some sterile gauze and applied a small bandage.

"You are officially a fisherman when you've had a hook removed in this manner. I, christen you, Sir Jeff, the fisherman," she said. She tapped him on the top of his head with her fly rod.

Jeff had been embarrassed, but now the sting seemed to be worth it.

"I feel like you knighted me, fair Princess," he joked.

His next cast, Jeff caught another fish, but it escaped after a tussle. His next cast caught a limb.

By this time they were all laughing.

Archie spoke, "Time for a sandwich. Tim, you hungry?"

"I'll say," Tim came running.

Lydia opened the canvas cooler and removed the wrapped sandwiches. Vera had placed huge slabs of ham between slices of bread. Some also contained cheese, mayonnaise or mustard. Tim took a cheese, Archie a mustard, cheese and ham. Lydia and Jeff took those that were left.

They all sat on a big boulder at the water's edge.

"Why does food always taste good outside?" Jeff asked.

"I think it's the mountain air. It makes you so hungry, anything tastes good," she said.

Lydia held up samples of beverages."Looks like bottles of lemonade, water or iced tea."

"I'll take the lemonade," Tim said.

Archie and Jeff each selected a bottle of water.

"Eat all you can. If we don't eat it, we have to pack it out and I have a feeling we're going to be very tired, very soon," Archie said.

They all tried, but soon could hold no more.

"Sorry, Archie, that's my limit," Jeff said.

Tim looked at Dixie. "Give her some bread." Archie looked at the dog drooling as she politely looked at them on the rock.

"Oh shot, give her a whole sandwich!" Archie said.

Lydia looked at Archie, "Are you sure? That's a hunk of meat there."

"I'm sure. Vera will be upset if we don't clean it all up and you heard us, we're all full."

Jeff and Tim smiled.

Tim flopped to his back."This is great. I haven't had so much fun fishing, since . . . Daddy took me."

The group became quiet.

Lydia looked off up the mountain.

Jeff bowed his head after he saw pain on her face.

Archie blew his nose in his big red handkerchief.

"We've about got enough fish but we can all cast a few more times. Then we need to head back so I can clean these and Vera can get them on to cook," Archie said.

After they caught two more fish, the group gathered

their gear and fell into line. There was little conversation as they walked back down the mountain.

Lydia spoke as they neared the cabin.

"We'll hit the showers, put on clean clothes and be down after while. Tell Vera I've got cole slaw, hush puppy mix, and a chocolate cake. We'll see you later. Thanks Archie and Pastor Jeff, we had a good time," Lydia said.

"Thanks," Tim repeated.

Refreshed by their showers, Lydia and Tim walked down the mountain carrying their bounty. Dixie bounded along beside the pair.

Archie had filleted the fish and Vera prepared a delicious fish dinner. With Lydia's additions, they enjoyed a great meal.

For some reason, appetites had returned and all ate well.

The group were quiet, content, and enjoyed the peaceful ending of the day after their successful venture.

Toward dusk, Pastor Jeff walked Tim, Dixie and Lydia back up the mountain.

As they left, Vera smiled at Archie. "I think those four are headed for some real happiness."

Archie looked after them. "It's about due."

When they arrived at the cabin, Tim took Dixie on their regular night patrol around the perimeters of their property.

Lydia and Pastor Jeff seated themselves on the deck chairs with big sighs of contentment.

"With a full stomach and lots of exercise, I'm beat," Lydia said. "The altitude is higher here, we're always tired for a week or so."

"Me too, but look at Tim and Dixie, they've got energy yet to burn," he said.

"Just wait, when they hit their beds, they'll be out like lights," Lydia said.

"That goes with being young. Ever watch a litter of puppies? They tussle, then collapse. It's fun to see," Pastor Jeff commented.

A comfortable silence settled over the pair. Only their eyes moved as they watched Tim and Dixie's progress over the lawn and stone wall.

Finally, Lydia turned to Pastor Jeff. "May I ask you a question, Rev. Boyd?"

"Yes, Mrs. Thayer. I may not have an answer, but fire at will."

"Don't call me, Mrs. Thayer. I hear that all the time. Sometimes I just want to be plain ole Lydia."

"Only if you'll drop the Reverend and call me Jeff," he said.

"Agreed, Jeff," Lydia said.

"Now, Lydia, what's your question?"

"Is this big bull elk a messenger from God, or a fluke?" she asked.

"Let me get the facts. He appears only after the hunting season for you and your son. For me, he appeared when I was totally at the bottom and saw no way up."

"Yes," she nodded.

"He came more than once to me at a different time of year, but you never see him when you're here all summer, or any other time?"

Lydia nodded again.

"You never saw him before your husband died?"

"No."

"He came right at the time of your husband's death?"

"Within a few minutes. We weren't looking right at the time, but at least very soon after Scott's last breath," Lydia said.

"Has Archie or Vera seen him?"

"No," she replied.

"Lydia, add all this up. What do you think?" Jeff asked.

"I don't know. It all seems very strange. I can't explain all this. I do know, several things," she said.

"And what do you know?" he asked.

"We feel better after we see him. We always find peace when he visits. He doesn't act like your average normal old bull. They are usually quite reclusive and wise, not appearing to humans. Definitely not in someone's own yard. They don't hang around for a hand-out either. If they were to come into our yard, normally it would be at night when no one would see them."

"Do you believe in miracles?" he asked.

"Yes, I believe I do," she said.

"Do you believe God could send any kind of messenger He chose?" Jeff asked gently.

"That's what I tell Tim," she said.

"But do you believe it?" he asked.

"Yes, I do believe God sent this particular elk to help us in a difficult time. Whether God caused it naturally, or in some supernatural way, I don't suppose I need to know," she answered.

"Lydia, that's what I believe too. I was as low as one can get. The thought of suicide crossed my mind. That was a method I don't approve for solving problems, but it came to me as a temptation. I had to recall conversations I'd had with others who had someone in their family commit suicide. Apparently that is the worst thing one can do to their own family. The families don't seem to ever recover entirely. I couldn't stand the thought of doing that to my parents and other extended family. At that time, the thought of hurting my family and those who trusted me, was the only thing that kept me from that temptation."

He continued, "I don't believe God intends for us to take our life into our own hands and out of His. He can handle any situation, without our interference. He'll lead us, if He wishes us to go in certain directions. We must have the faith to be patient and see where that will go. I had to fight a Spiritual war against the thought and it was not leaving my mind," Jeff held up a finger, "until I saw your elk. He gazed into my eyes and I felt something, almost electrical pour a message into my brain."

"Can you tell me the message?" she asked.

"The message was, "I am not finished with you. I love you, I have a ministry for you, and the job is yours alone. You are my servant, I made you for this task, go and do my work,'" Jeff bowed his head. "How could I do otherwise?"

"Like Tim says, Wow!" that was profound, but I understand. Tim and I were very sad. This bull elk came. He seemed to look into our hearts and we felt good about Scott's eternal life. We found peace," a tear slid down Lydia's face.

Jeff laid his hand along her jaw line and wiped her tear with his thumb.

"I'm very glad you found some peace, no matter how God choose to send it. He can use anything and anyone to carry His message," Jeff said.

"I'm very glad you also found peace and purpose. I'm glad you didn't kill yourself. I can see how God can use you. You are like Vera, you can help others handle losses and you can assist them in their journey toward Christ. Thank you for helping me," Lydia whispered.

"Thank you, Lydia, for providing a way for me to return to life and purpose," he sighed.

"We're a pair, aren't we?" Lydia smiled.

"We are. Is it possible God placed us together for a purpose too?" he asked.

She looked at the intensity in his eyes. "I don't know,

but I'm going to pray about it. Especially for Tim's sake, I don't want to make any mistakes. I don't want to do that to him," she said.

"I think we need some time. May I come see you and Tim this winter?" he asked.

"I need to pray about it first, but I am thinking it could be possible. I'll ask Tim what he thinks about it too. I'll try to give you an answer as soon as we decide. I'll write you later, if we can't decide before you have to leave," Lydia promised.

"I need to pray too. Your answer is good enough for me. I must get back to Archie and Vera's. I'd like to see you and Tim before I leave tomorrow, if that's possible?" Jeff asked.

"That will be fine. Do you wish to come here? You could have lunch with us, or we can come down to Archie and Vera's," Lydia said.

"I'd like to come here. Even though it belongs to you, I love this place. I feel God here, more than I can many places. Do you feel Him?" Jeff asked.

"Yes, especially at dawn or sunset, when the tops of the mountains are aglow. When His light bursts on the scene. or when His light goes behind the peaks at evening. I do feel His special presence. I can feel it in the city, but never as closely as here. The whole place stands for a lot for us. It's a good place to be Spiritually, emotionally, and physically. We feel very healthy when we're here. Can you understand that?" she asked.

She started, "I don't know why I said we feel healthier, Scott certainly loved it and he got sick and died here."

"Perhaps Scott would have died much sooner had he not had God's creation. His being here and enjoying his life and family may have prolonged his life beyond what he could have had in the city, or under more stress," Jeff said.

"According to what you've told me, you and Scott had a very close relationship. That had to be good for his health."

Lydia hesitated. "This may sound strange, but while he was ill, was the best and worst time of our whole marriage." She looked away.

"I'm afraid I don't understand," Jeff questioned.

"Scott was able to spend uninterrupted time with us. We all talked in a way, we never had before. I never felt closer to him than I did during his illness. That was the good part," she said.

"I can guess the worst,"Jeff whispered.

Lydia didn't say anything, but looked off to the mountain.

After a moment, he said,"My wife. . . and daughter didn't get time to say good by. I think that was part of why I was so desolate when they were gone. Had we the time to really talk, we could have told each other how much I loved her and our daughter. I suppose that's what the psychologists call closure. I had to work it out for myself and sometimes those feelings still creep up on me," Jeff said. "I don't want to be morbid. I have found a balance in my life and I have moved on, but that doesn't take a thing from them. I still love them dearly and can't wait to see them again, but it isn't God's timing, and I'll have to see how that turns out."

They were quiet, both cocooned within their own thoughts.

Finally, Jeff took a deep breath and stood. He walked to the railing, "I can certainly understand why you say you feel healthier here, the air is pure and cold. There is a peace and lack of stress we couldn't find most places, but I think a lot of the Spiritual and emotional peace is in His creation. The peace gives one time to meditate and feel God's presence. When in the hubbub of the city or the world, His voice is sometimes blocked out. He can make Himself heard in the city, but we don't allow His voice. We can't hear the Voice for the noise."

He smiled, "Some say, 'You can't see the trees for the forest', but I'd change it to what I just said. If you get close enough you can hear or see God, no matter where you are at the moment."

Letting Go

After Tim went to bed, Lydia felt melancholy. She wandered around the cabin looking at it in a different way.

Scott, I'm glad everyone appreciates your workmanship on our cabin. I still love it here.

I'm sorry to tell you, but if you can't be here, I'd like for Jeff to at least visit. Am I wrong to want that? You were my friend and advisor, besides being my husband and all that meant to us. Help me know what to do next.

After a couple of hours, she drifted off before the fireplace wrapped in a blanket, with Scott's pillow under her head.

Lydia drifted into a dream. Scott came to her. He spoke, "Remember, I told you not to look back. Find Joy for you and Tim. Be Happy!"

She awoke with a jerk. Her cheeks were wet. She felt a wet tongue. Dixie was beside her.

"Good dog. You take good care of us. It's okay girl, go back to Tim. I'm okay. Do you need to go out?"

Dixie looked toward the door, then clumped back up the stairs. Lydia heard her nails on the floor overhead, until she heard a thump on the floor when Dixie lay back down beside Tim's bed.

Lydia could not go back to sleep. She got their Bible from the bedroom and turned on a light. She reread the passages of Scripture Scott had used when he directed her toward a future without him.

He knew there might come a time when I'd find

someone I could love. He tried his best to make me see that
would be best for me and Tim. But it makes me feel. . . awful.
It's a final good-by I never wanted. I have to turn loose of my
husband, on earth, in order to love another. Oh, God, help me.
I don't know what to do.

Moving On

Lydia and Tim spent several evenings with Jeff when he came to visit them at Gunnison. He didn't come often, due to his work schedule, but he showed attentiveness to both of them.

Lydia realized Jeff was moving closer to them with each visit.

One Friday evening he leaned in close and kissed her.

Afterwards, Lydia was in a pensive and confused mood.

"Lydia, did I move too fast?" he asked quietly.

"I don't know. I'm torn. Have you been able to put your wife's memory away?" she asked.

"Yes, and no. I still love her, but I know she'd want me to move on. My life is lonely. I'm a family man, without a family," he said.

"Do you come here because we're a family, or do you really care about us?" she asked.

"I really, really care," he said.

Lydia could see it in his eyes. "I'm sorry, I shouldn't have asked that."

"Why not?" he asked.

"I don't know how to say it. I don't know if I've put Scott away." Her voice hitched, " I don't want . . . to put him away."

He looked at the tears in her eyes.

"I don't think we'll ever not love them, but it's different now. We've mourned a long time. The Bible says there's a time to weep, a time to mourn, but there are other seasons. It's all right to find joy and move on to the next step," he counseled.

Lydia looked into his eyes with some hope dawning in her own.

"In his last weeks, Scott told me he wanted Tim and I to find Joy. It's strange you used the same words," she said.

"Maybe not. Maybe God put that in my mind," Jeff said.

"I don't know." She buried her face in her hands.

Jeff gathered her in a brotherly hug. "That's all right. God has time, I have time. He'll let us know what is to happen next."

She quieted in his arms.

After a time, Jeff set her away from him.

"It's getting late, I'd better get back to the motel. I'll come by and take you and Tim to breakfast in the morning before I take off for home."

"Okay." She looked so pitiful Jeff kissed her on the forehead.

"I hope you can get some sleep," he said.

"I'm not sure that will happen," she sighed.

"You have my cell number. If you need to talk during the night, please do," he said.

"You won't want to hear from me at three AM," she said.

"You'd be surprised. I like to hear from you anytime. Your troubles are my troubles. I'm here for you," he said.

"You're a good man. I wish I didn't have such mixed feelings." Her tears started again.

"Come here." He hugged her against his chest. "I am accustomed to taking on the problems of others. Yours have become my problems. Let me carry some of your burden for you. Let God carry the rest," Jeff said. "However, you should know, for the record, I don't hug any other ladies I counsel." He smiled and was able to draw a smile from Lydia.

"Okay, I promise I'll get some sleep and I don't think I'll call you at three," she said.

They laughed.

"You don't promise?"

"No, I don't like to break my word." She stood straighter. "You're good for me, Jeff. You take me out of myself."

"And that's a good thing?" he asked.

"Yes, maybe I'm examining things too minutely when I should be relaxing and enjoying. I should find the Joy, as Scott said."

"He gave good advice. Wish I could have met him," he said.

"Me too," Lydia breathed.

Jeff looked down, he fidgeted. "I'll tell you a secret, one time in the middle of the night, I looked at Tim's one-week video. I saw Scott's heart in his eyes. I liked him. He was a good man."

"He was and he loved that boy!" Lydia said.

"He loved that mom too." Jeff put his finger to his lips and onto the tip of her nose. "Night. See you and Tim for breakfast."

"Okay," she smiled through her tears.

New Family

Before Easter, Jeff asked Tim for permission to marry his mother.

Tim replied, "You bet. What took you so long? I've

wanted you in our family ever since we went fishing. Dixie and I like you."

The whole family went to meet with all their parents and former in laws.

The families approved.

Scott's parents gathered Jeff, Lydia and Tim together. Scott's father spoke, "We're very glad you have found each other. We want a new family for Scott's family and you can make that family. We love each of you."

Dixie woofed.

"You too, Dixie!"

They all chuckled.

The families joined forces.

God's New Messenger

The year Tim was ten years of age, his little sister, Joy Elizabeth Boyd arrived at dawn on the day after the elk season ended. The family wasn't on the mountain to see if God's Messenger came, but the that messenger was no longer needed. A different messenger had come into their lives.

Jeff called all four sets of grandparents on the day of Joy Elizabeth's birth.

"Would you all like to come meet your new grand daughter?" was the message he relayed to all.

The older couples communicated well. They spaced their visits. The last occurred at Christmas vacation.

Scott's parents went with the younger family to Scott's Mountain for the last of the four visits.

Scott's mother spoke to both of the adults, "We loved Scott more than most can imagine loving a son, but we also love you, Lydia and Jeff. We know Scott is pleased that you both will find happiness with Tim and Joy Elizabeth. We're so happy you can keep Scott's Mountain and can enjoy the learning and play times the family can have here. That was what Scott wanted for everyone, that they could enjoy nature and God's creation. He wanted it preserved for all generations. Be happy, carry on with both your ministries. That is the very best thing you can do to please God. . .," her voice broke, "and Scott."

Lydia stepped to give Scott's mother a hug. His father stepped to her and joined arms around the two women. All their cheeks were wet.

Jeff cleared his throat, "God's blessings on all of us. Thank you Father, and Scott."

Afterglow

Dixie continued to watch her family on the trails in the mountain with Joy in a backpack on one of her parents' backs, or from a spot under the umbrella at the beach where Joy Elizabeth played in the sand beside her mother.

Dixie didn't need to move as quickly with the little one barely learning to walk. Tim and his new father, Jeff, were the active ones now.

Each summer and at vacation time, they came to the cabin and walked the mountain in search of rest and relaxation. The whole family brightened when they returned to the mountains.

They never again saw the magnificent old bull elk, despite the fact, they looked every time they returned to Scott's Mountain. They felt God's presence without the embodiment of the big elk and in God's plan they would lean on each other.

Sweet little Joy seemed to be God's New Messenger for the Boyd family. They assumed God sent other messengers to other families to assure they survived the terrors of life in their world. Their own cup was full, God had provided for them. They kept their eyes on Him and His purpose for each of their lives.

In the years to come, due to the efforts of Tim's father, his grandparents, researchers from Scott's alma mater, and those over the world who believed in the conservation of God's natural resources and creation, Tim and Joy's own children would enjoy Scott's Mountain and later generations of the same plant and animal species.

Perhaps the old Messenger's progeny were amongst those that roamed the Rocky Mountain forests of evergreens and aspen on Scott's Mountain.

The End